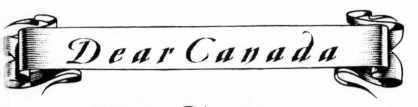

NO SAFE HARBOUR

∞

THE HALIFAX EXPLOSION DIARY
OF CHARLOTTE BLACKBURN

BY JULIE LAWSON

Scholastic Canada Ltd.

Halifax, Nova Scotia,
1917

Behind the lines, somewhere in France

July 30, 1917

Dear Charlotte,

If you're reading this, you'll see that the first page of your diary has already been taken. Some cheapskate brother, eh? You can tear it out if you like. I bought two of these diaries, one for you (being the writer in the family) and one for me, and I'll reserve my first page for you. Okay? Then we'll be square.

Here's the deal. I record my life in the trenches. You record your life on the home front. One day we'll sit down together and compare notes. I promise I won't look at the entries you mark "secret," so you can be honest. Don't bury your feelings behind the blackout curtains. Shout them out bravely.

You know the song you and Duncan can't sing for laughing? We're bunked up in huts near there and

I'm practising the few words I know of the parlez-vous. *Like* bonjour, merci *and* au revoir. *It's good to go into the local cafés and spend some francs on fresh eggs and chips. We'll be back in the trenches eating bully beef before you know it. Ugh!*

How's Kirsty? Is she still scaring off all the neighbourhood cats? Are you and Duncan giving her lots of exercise? How about old Haggarty? Still helping him out on the milk run?

Gee I miss you and the folks. I've been blowing the odd kiss at the mademoiselles, but don't tell my Jane! I'll blow you a kiss on September 26 in honour of your birthday. 12 years old!? I won't recognize you!

Keep up the knitting! A new pair of socks is a prized possession here in the mudholes.

Your loving brother,
Luke

Wednesday, September 26, 1917

9:00 p.m.

Here I am, writing in my new diary. Is there a proper way to do it? One page per day? A few lines about noteworthy events? Something about the weather? (Clear sky, westerly winds, warmer than yesterday.) I don't suppose it matters, so long as I write something every day, even if there's nothing much to write about. And if I pick the same time every day, it will become a habit.

Now's a good time, before Ruth and Edith come to bed and I still have the room to myself. Privacy! A prized possession, here on the Home Front.

This diary was a big surprise. It was in the package that arrived last month, but Mum's kept it hidden until this morning. She's good at keeping secrets. And Luke's good at secret codes. The song he mentioned is "Mademoiselle from Armentières," so that's where he must have been camped. Where is he now, I wonder.

His letter was an even bigger surprise. He usually writes a "Dear Folks" letter, not a special one just for me. But tear out the page? Never! Although it does have a few dirty blotches.

At first I was afraid they were bloodstains. Was

it Luke's blood? Had he been injured? I was some worried until Duncan assured me it was plain old mud. Because blood would be more of a rusty colour.

Duncan asked why Luke hadn't sent *him* a diary, since it's his birthday, too. Oh, gosh, didn't he sound hurt and sulky. Not a bit like usual. He even threw in the fact that he's nine minutes older than me! As if I needed reminding.

I assured him that Luke hadn't forgotten him, because what about all the swell postcards he'd sent. Besides, Luke knows that Duncan would never write in a diary. He'd rather draw pictures.

Well instead of agreeing with me, Duncan pouts and says, "I would so write in it."

So I promised to give him a diary for Christmas, and said he could write in mine the same way Luke had. That cheered him up.

"But no more than a page," I insisted, and made him promise not to tell the others. I don't want the whole family taking over my diary.

He agreed and took the diary away to write something in secret.

Now that I've got it back, it's tempting to flip ahead and see what he wrote, but I won't. Why not? Because it'll be much more fun to find his entry a few days or weeks from now. Then I'll really be surprised!

We had a swell birthday, except for Luke not being here. Mum made a cake and Edith gave us a bag of butterscotch taffy. Ruth wasn't late for supper for a change so she and Dad didn't get into their usual row. She even cleared the table and washed the dishes without being told. Life was peaceful on the Blackburn Home Front.

After supper we played cards. Edith made cocoa. Right on cue, Dad started to quote the cocoa ad, and we all chimed in, "More food value than a cup of bouillon."

Lucky for us that cocoa's cheaper than bouillon!

After cocoa, Edith played the piano and Dad played his accordion and we sang a few songs. Mum always picks "Keep the Home Fires Burning" even though it makes her cry. Duncan and I played "Pack Up Your Troubles" — me on the piano and Duncan on his harmonica — and Kirsty started to howl! We didn't sound *that* bad. Then we sang "Mademoiselle from Armentières," because Luke's right, it *always* makes us laugh. *Mademoiselle from Armentières, she hasn't been kissed in forty years, hinky-dinky parlez-voo!* Which means, "Hinky-dinky do you speak?" What kind of nonsense is that? As usual, Mum corrected our pronunciation. "*Armentières* doesn't rhyme with *years*," she says. "It rhymes with *air*."

Well we like it sounding silly!

Oh, no. I just spotted Ruth going into the bathroom. Better put this away before she comes in and demands to see what I've written. So just one more paragraph.

I wonder what scenes from the Home Front will fill these pages. Nothing tragic or sad, I hope. But no matter what happens, if I feel the urge to hide my true thoughts and feelings, I'll re-read Luke's words and bravely plunge ahead. Not that I'll have thoughts and feelings worth hiding, but now that I'm twelve, who knows?

(Luke, when you're reading this, I hope my first entry isn't too long.)

Thursday, September 27

I haven't even had breakfast and here I am, starting a new entry. So much for writing at the same time every day. I can't wait that long!

Right now I'm curled up on the landing beside the stained glass window. The house is warm and cozy. Dad's stoked the furnace and Mum's making porridge. They're talking in the kitchen.

Ruth is muttering in the bedroom, trying to find something she's misplaced (as usual).

Edith's in the living room, practising for her Conservatory of Music exam. She's playing my favourite piece, a waltz by Chopin. It sounds perfect.

Now Kirsty's barking at the back door and Dad's yelling at her to pipe down. She whines a complaint but does as she's told. Good dog.

The sun's shining through the window, making coloured patterns on the page and on my hand. Rose and green and amber. I feel as if I'm tucked inside a glowing jewel.

I love this window because Dad gave it to Mum when they were married. "I can't afford to buy you the kind of home you're used to," he said. "But I can afford a lovely window for my lovely bride. And when our ship comes in . . . "

"We'll take the window with us," said Mum.

Of course I wasn't around to hear this conversation, but they've told the story so many times I might as well have been. Once I asked Mum what kind of home she was used to, before she married Dad. She said she couldn't remember. Well I wonder about that. She remembers going to a ladies' college in Boston and she remembers some of the French she learned when she went to Paris, but she can't remember her own *home?*

Maybe it was a castle! Wouldn't that be a story — how John Blackburn, the humble (and handsome) dry dock worker (now foreman) spied Lillian the Fair in her castle tower and rescued her from the clutches of a wicked king!

Now I have to have breakfast and get ready for the milk run. Haggarty will be here in no time.

Still Thursday, bedtime

Back to this morning. After breakfast I went outside and soon enough the milk wagon was stopping at our gate. I gave old Queenie a carrot and a kiss on the nose, then climbed up beside Haggarty.

He gives me a wink and says, "I wasn't expecting you this morning, seeing as you're a young lady of twelve now."

I had to laugh. Give up the milk run just because I'm twelve? Never! I feel right posh sitting high up on the driver's seat, especially when Haggarty lets me take the reins. I cluck my tongue and go Gee-up and Whoa even though Queenie's the one in control. And doesn't she know it!

Well off we go, with Kirsty bounding ahead or trailing behind, sniffing, exploring, greeting every dog as if she'd never set foot in the neighbourhood before.

Clip, clop, Queenie's hooves on the cinder streets, clang-clang the metal milk cans, swish-swash the fresh milk lapping the sides. I'm thirsty just thinking about it! Especially the thick rich cream on top.

Haggarty always gives me a cup of cream to sip on the route. He says I need fattening up. Mum says the same thing, but she doesn't give me all the cream at home.

The milk run's a fine way to pass the time between breakfast and school, and I wish I could do it more often. It's fun to greet the neighbours and give them a hand when they come out to fill their pitchers, and they ask about this and that, like how many socks I've knit for the Junior Red Cross and has my mum got over her migraine and what's the latest news from Luke.

The sad part of today was when Mrs. Mortimer came out for her two pints. She was dressed in black because yesterday she learned that her Tommy was killed in France. He went to school with Luke.

I meant to show Haggarty my diary this morning, and Luke's letter, but I forgot.

Better stop now. This entry's so long, my diary will be finished before October if I don't restrain myself. Long-winded, that's me.

Friday, September 28

Typical Friday.

Chores, breakfast, school.

Mental arithmetic drill, spelling test, round-robin reading, geography lesson, Mr. Barker blowing his top. Special Projects in the afternoon.

Knitting in Special Projects. Started a new contest with Muriel, Eva, Deirdre and some of the other girls. This time it's for a balaclava helmet.

Piano lesson after school. Misery. Miss Tebo cross because I haven't been practising. "Birthdays are no excuse!"

There you are, a short entry for once.

Saturday, September 29

Fed the chickens, brought in the eggs, helped Duncan muck out Billy the Pig's pen and dumped in a fresh load of scraps. He snorted happily, poor old Billy. I wish we could keep him as a pet, but he'll be fit for the table by Christmas.

After that we cleaned out the furnace and put the cinders in buckets for the collection wagon.

The rest of the day was fun. Took the trolley to town with Mum and Duncan. First we went shopping for Duncan's cadet uniform. Then, as a special treat for twelve-year-olds, Mum took us to the Corona Café for a mid-day dinner! For 25¢ you could get a dressed spring chicken (or cod or roast beef) with steamed potatoes, creamed carrots and a choice of desserts. We all chose the chicken dinner. For dessert I had tapioca pudding, Duncan had ice cream, Mum had raisin pie and we all had a taste of each other's. Duncan ate so much it's a wonder he didn't have to get a bigger-size uniform.

After lunch we went to the post office so I could mail a thank-you letter to Luke. I promised him I'd keep a daily record in my diary, even if some days are dull and uneventful.

Back at home we had a fashion parade with Duncan strutting around the house in his new uniform. Ruth played a sergeant, of course. Eyes right! Forward, march! Hup, two, three, four! Attennnnn — shun! She's some good at barking orders.

Mum was teary-eyed, watching Duncan play the soldier. She might have been thinking what I'm thinking — what if the war's still on when Duncan turns eighteen? What if he goes off to France like Luke?

Sunday, September 30

Church in the morning.

Sunday dinner after church.

Weather sunny and fair, so we spent the afternoon at Point Pleasant Park (everyone except Ruth). Lots of Sunday strollers.

Dad, Duncan and I walked along the beach and watched a tug opening the gate in the anti-submarine net. There was a convoy coming into the harbour so we watched that for a while. Then Dad lit a fire on the beach.

While Mum was boiling the kettle for tea and Edith was laying out the cloth, two soldiers came by and stopped to chat. They were nice and friendly so Mum invited them to join us.

Turns out they're from Winnipeg, and with the Army Medical Corps. Right now they're looking after the wounded that come off the ships, but in another two months they'll be sent overseas to work in a field hospital.

Duncan told them he'd just turned twelve so now he can join the Richmond School Cadet Corps. Oh didn't he go on about it, the uniforms and rifles and drills. The soldiers listened politely, but anyone could see they were more interested in talking to Edith. She can turn a soldier's head without even trying.

And wasn't Ruth sorry she hadn't gone with us! Especially when I told her that Charlie, one of the Winnipeg soldiers, is as handsome as her idol, Douglas Fairbanks!

Monday, October 1

Went down the tracks after school with Duncan and Carl and waited for the train. As soon as it came alongside we hollered and pretended to throw rocks at the engine, and Carl's dad pretended to be annoyed and threw coal at us from the tender. Then we put the coal in a sack and took it to Carl's house.

Carl's mum gave us a bit to bring home. We took it down the basement and put it in the coal scuttle. Secretly, so Mum and Dad won't know. They think it's stealing from the railway. But aren't they always complaining about the high price of coal? It's our way of helping out, and it's only a few little chunks.

Tuesday, October 2

Luke, when you're reading this, here's an example of what you're missing on the Home Front.

Today, after school. Mum, Ruth and I are sitting around the kitchen table, eating fresh-baked bread. (Duncan's outside feeding Billy the Pig.)

Mum *always* wants me to eat more, even though I eat as much as anyone else. "You're too thin," she says. "People will think I'm not feeding you properly. Here, have another slice of bread. Look at Ruth, how nicely she's filled out."

"You'll never get a husband, scrawny thing like you," Ruth says with her mouth full.

A *husband?* I'm only twelve!

Mum says it's the worrying that makes me thin, and the food that's meant to fill me out gets eaten up by nervous energy. "You're wasting away," she says. "We need to fatten you up."

"Why? So you can slaughter me like Billy the Pig?" Ha ha.

A rare attempt at humour but didn't it fall flat. Mum gave me her "don't be cheeky" look. Ruth rolled her eyes in disgust. If Ruth had said it, Mum would have laughed.

Weather clear and cool. Leaves turning colour.

Wednesday, October 3

A letter from Luke, written August 24.

He says he's fine, and we're not to worry, but it's grim, this letter, the way he describes the open stretch of ground called No Man's Land — the mud and shell holes, the smell of dead bodies —

where a line of Huns on one side faces a line of Allies on the other. All of them stuck in their trenches until the order goes out — "Over the top!" — and the killing begins.

The letter says he's just finished a tour of trench duty, so he's safe for now, behind the lines. Three or four days on the front line might not sound long, he tells us, but every minute feels like a year, with the "earth-shaking bombardments" and "fireworks night after night," and "no picnic" when it's raining, which is most of the time. And the place is overrun with giant rats.

He has to do chores, too. Horrible chores like digging latrines or draining a trench with the mud to his knees.

Sometimes the front lines are so close, you can hear a Hun sneeze. That's what Luke says, but I think he's joking. Luke with the sense of humour.

Mum gave me the letter so I could copy a bit in my diary:

The next parcel you send, could you tuck in a box of sleep? A good forty winks would be a luxury. If it's not the fireworks keeping us awake, it's the itching caused by the blasted lice.

More than anything, keep sending your prayers.

I wish we *could* send him a box of sleep.

Showers all day and a cold wind.

Milk run this morning. Haggarty said that Princess's puppies should be born some time this week.

Eva came over after school with her knitting. I told her what Luke had written about No Man's Land and how sometimes you could hear a Hun sneeze. I said *Hun* without thinking and right away felt bad because of Eva's dad being a German. Eva didn't mind. She said it was a good thing her dad came to Canada, because otherwise *he* might have been one of the soldiers that Luke heard sneezing. Except that he's too old to go to war, and now that he's a Canadian, he'd be fighting on *our* side.

While we were knitting we made up limericks like we did last year, but we only had time for one:

There was a young girl called Muriel
Who sang while eating her cereal
But alas she choked
On a very high note
And that was the end of poor Muriel.

Eva thought up most of it. We gave up on her own name because we couldn't think of anything that rhymes with Eva.

Almost forgot. Last night I had a terrible dream about No Man's Land. The "Over the top!" cry went out and I leapt out of a trench and charged across the muddy ground trying not to get hit. Then I saw that I hadn't put on my boots or my helmet and I'd forgotten my rifle and bayonet. I turned to go back, but I couldn't move. The mud was sucking me down. I was thinking, Mum will be furious when she sees my clean dress covered in mud. I'd only put it on that morning and where was my uniform? I was some relieved to wake up. Girls can't be soldiers and I've never even seen a No Man's Land or a trench, so why would I have such a horrible dream? Worrying about Luke, I suppose.

There were birds in the dream. I wonder where they go during a battle. Where do they build their nests when all the trees have been blasted away? What happens to the little animals like squirrels and rabbits?

Friday, October 5

Mr. Barker yelled at me because I lost my place in reading. My own fault. I was trying to find a word that rhymes with Eva. Came up with "fever."

Told the girls in Special Projects and they all said, "That doesn't rhyme."

But ha ha on them, because it rhymes when you pronounce it the British way. So we said it like Mr. Barker (but quietly) and made up this limerick:

There once was a girl called Eva
Who came down with a terrible fevah
She turned a bright red
From her toes to her head
But got cured by a bath full of vinegah.

Muriel wanted us to change *her* limerick so she could be cured at the end like Eva. Gosh, it's only a silly rhyme, but we told her we'd try.

We were going to make up some more after school but I had to go to my piano lesson. Miss Tebo rapped my knuckles with her ruler because I kept making the same mistakes on my scales. I must have been scowling when I went outside because the student who goes after me said, "Cheer up, Charlotte. It'll be better next week."

I'm too shy to ask her name because she's much older than I am, around Edith's age. She's awfully nice. Especially the way she brings a treat for Kirsty every week. No wonder Kirsty likes going to piano lessons!

Saturday, October 6

Went to the matinee at the Casino Theatre and saw a spectacular motion picture called *Joan the Woman.* It was a birthday treat from Edith. I love being twelve. I never thought we'd be so spoiled.

The picture's about Joan of Arc, and it's told in the form of a dream. There's a French soldier in the trenches who's been asked to give his life for the good of the army. He's trying to decide what to do when suddenly he uncovers an ancient sword. The moment he takes hold of the sword he has a vision of Joan of Arc and the ancient battle in France and he sees how she died for her country. So he follows her example and does the same. It's heroic but sad.

Duncan's favourite part was the Battle of the Towers, when the British were besieged by the French. Soldiers were falling off the walls of the fortress into a moat and their bodies were bristling with arrows.

I liked everything, except for the part when Joan was burned at the stake. I had to close my eyes.

Edith's favourite part was the romance between Joan and her British beau. We teased her on the way home and asked if the romance made her think of the Winnipeg soldiers we met last week. Her face turned so red I'm sure the answer was yes!

I wonder what makes things change. Hundreds of years ago the British and French were mortal enemies. Now they're fighting on the same side and Germany's *their* mortal enemy.

Of course it's all the Kaiser's fault, but it's hard to understand. Especially since our King George and the Kaiser are related. Cousins, I think.

Sunday, October 7

Thanksgiving Sunday and St. Mark's was beautiful. Cornucopias and baskets spilling out with squashes, gourds, apples and pumpkins, cornstalks and sheaves of wheat and flowers, and everything red and yellow and orange.

We sang my favourite hymn and it's still singing inside my head:

Come, ye thankful people, come, raise the song of harvest home
All is safely gathered in, ere the winter storms begin . . .

I love those two lines, even though I don't understand the "harvest home" part. Dad says you don't have to understand every last bit of a song or a poem. The important thing is how it makes you feel. Well today all the hymns made me feel thankful. Especially that one.

Roast goose for dinner, and this time it was Dad urging me to have some more. "Let's fatten you up!" he says.

I obliged by having two big helpings of Mum's pumpkin pie.

Monday, October 8

Thanksgiving Day and a holiday. Dad and Duncan went hunting.

Wrote a letter to Luke. Ran up Fort Needham with Kirsty, raced around the top of the hill, then over to Haggarty's farm. No puppies yet. Tea and gossip with Mrs. Haggarty.

Practised the piano and played duets with Edith. She asked if I'd like to be a stenographer one day, since I had such "nimble" fingers. I told her I might, but only if I worked in the same office as her. Then we could play duets on our typewriters.

Weather clear and cool.

Tuesday, October 9

Deirdre was away today. Last month her brother was wounded and lost an arm. He was going to be shipped home to recover, but Deirdre's family found out yesterday that he died in a hospital in England. He was eighteen.

Every weekend when the newpaper prints a Casualty List we always recognize some of the names. Especially Mum and Dad — they may not know the boy himself, but they usually know his parents or a brother or sister or some other relative, from work or church or the neighbourhood.

The Casualty List is long and there are lots of categories. Infantry, Artillery, Wounded Severe, Wounded Slightly, Died of Wounds, Reported Wounded, Gas Poisoning, Gas Poison Severe, Gassed and Wounded, Killed, Missing, Killed in Action.

Duncan never looks at the Casualty List. He says I shouldn't either because it only makes me worry. But now that I've written down the words I feel as if I'm trapping bad luck on the page and keeping it away from Luke. That's because sometimes, when you *imagine* the worst, it doesn't happen.

I'm right sad for Deirdre.

Wednesday, October 10

Three weeks till Hallowe'en. Duncan and I are dressing up as each other. We look enough alike and we're about the same height. Duncan's not as scrawny as me, but I'll tuck extra newspapers under my coat and no one will know the difference.

I'm going to wear Duncan's brown pants, long black stockings and brown tweed coat and he's going to wear my plaid coat and the blue serge skirt that's still too big for me. Ruth's daring him to wear her pink corset. Duncan, in a girl's corset? Never!

Edith says she'll pin up my hair and tuck it under Duncan's cap.

Thursday, October 11

Princess had five puppies on Tuesday night. Haggarty says they're the spitting image of Kirsty when she was a pup. Can't wait to see them. I'll take Kirsty so she can see her mother and her new brothers and sisters.

School uneventful, except that Brian got the strap for fidgeting. *Again.*

Came home and practised my scales over and over until everyone begged me to stop. If my knuckles get rapped tomorrow it won't be my fault.

Friday, October 12

Special Projects today and I took my knitting as usual. Everything was fine until I felt a tug and couldn't pull any more wool. I thought there was a tangle or something, but when I reached into my basket, the ball of wool wasn't there. So I turned around and wouldn't you know it, there's Carl with a big guilty grin. He'd taken the wool from my basket and tied it to his desk.

I gave him a right good scowl, I was that mad. I'd almost caught up to Muriel for first place in our balaclava contest, and if it wasn't for Carl I might have outknitted her today.

At supper, Edith said that Carl must be sweet on me to go to all that trouble to get my attention.

I pulled a face and groaned, but secretly I was pleased, until Ruth went and spoiled things. "Carl, sweet on Charlotte?" she says. "He must be a blind fool, or stupid as a bag of hammers."

Luke, when you're reading this, here's a secret you can read — I *hate* Ruth. I'd never say it out loud, but it's true, even though she is my sister.

Mum knows we don't get along. She says we'll grow out of it and one day we'll be the best of friends. Ruth and me, friends? Never! Because as much as I hate her, she hates me more.

Here's the proof. When I was little, Ruth told

me that Mum didn't want me. "She was right thrilled when Duncan was born," Ruth said to me. "But when you came along, Mum cried, 'Oh, no! Not another one!'"

Duncan says Ruth is only making it up, but when I see how Mum favours her, I think it must be true.

Then there's the story that Mum loves to tell. Remember, Luke? That when Ruth saw Duncan and me for the first time, she pointed at Duncan and said, "Can we keep this one, and send the other one back?"

Everyone laughs when Mum tells this story, but I don't think it's funny. Even though Mum says she wouldn't send me back for all the world.

Where is back? Where was I before I was born? Is it a place like heaven, where you go back to after you die?

Luke, if you're still reading this, remember when Ruth almost drowned me? She said it was an accident, that I slid underwater in the bath when she was supposed to be watching me. If you hadn't come in at just the right moment, who knows?

Now, what got me thinking about that? Oh, what Ruth said about Carl. Well here's another secret. I *am* sweet on Carl. What can I do to get *his* attention?

I love writing in my diary. Maybe feelings are stronger and more honest when you put them on a page. It's better than having them run around loose in your head.

One more thing about today. I played my scales perfectly. Miss Tebo was pleased, and when I played my pieces she said I was "following in Edith's footsteps." A rare compliment!

The same friendly girl was there today and I told her that she was right. My lesson was better this week. Even for Kirsty, because today she got two treats.

Saturday, October 13

Chores this morning. Thought of Luke digging latrines, so didn't complain about dusting.

Went down to the harbour after lunch so Duncan could sketch the *Highflyer*. He'd only just started when who should we see but Ruth and her friend Hilda. They didn't see us, so we played Spy and followed them around. Had to pinch ourselves to keep from laughing, the way they were giggling and making eyes at the sailors and the sailors weren't even noticing. Those sailors must have been blind — or right smart!

After a while it got boring, spying on Ruth, so Duncan picked out a soldier and we tailed him all the way to the Empire Theatre. We couldn't get in to see the picture because we didn't have any money, so we spied on three sailors instead.

They weren't that interesting. They smoked cigarettes and whistled at girls and walked as if they were still on a rolling deck. They were speaking a foreign language so we couldn't eavesdrop, but we had fun imitating them (except for the whistling at girls), until an old lady stopped us, right on the sidewalk, and told us to show some respect.

Duncan apologized in his usual charming way, said we'd meant no harm, and told her about our brother in the trenches. Next thing you know she's patting his shoulder and talking about her grandson who was wounded in France.

I didn't say anything, just stood there feeling guilty and ashamed. The sailors will be leaving Halifax before long, and they might not even make it across the Atlantic. Their ship could be hit by a German submarine and they could all be lost at sea. I'll never make fun of sailors again.

It was a year ago that Luke and the boys from the 85th "Red Feather" Battalion marched off to war, their kilts swirling and the bagpipes playing. Down Pier 2, onto the *Olympic* and at dusk they sailed away.

We talked about it at supper tonight. How

there wasn't a dry eye on the pier, watching them go, and how handsome Luke looked, how proud and brave. And how worried we'd been about the *Olympic*, because, being a sister ship of the *Titanic*, she might be bad luck.

Well, by the time supper was finished, there wasn't a dry eye at the table.

I hope I don't dream about trenches or No Man's Land.

Sunday, October 14

Sunday School in the morning. I got a bookmark for naming all the books in the Old Testament. Genesis, Exodus, Leviticus, Numbers, Deuteronomy and so on. The bookmark has a picture of Jesus talking to a group of children. It says, *Suffer the little children to come unto me, for of such is the Kingdom of Heaven.* I should know what it means, but I don't. Why do little children have to suffer? Why is there suffering in heaven?

Clear and cool today.

Monday, October 15

Today we had to write a composition called "The Symphony of Autumn." Mine started like this: *The leaves look crisp and spirited and happy dressed up in their new fall clothes while they wait for their conductor, Mr. Wind, to scatter them over the town.*

I used lots of colourful words like blazing scarlet, fiery orange, majestic bronze and gleaming gold. I hope I get an A.

Muriel came over after school — she brought Ethel along too — and we took our knitting into the playhouse. Ethel gurgled happily in her pram while we chatted and clicked away. After the war, when there's no more knitting for soldiers, we're going to hook a rug for the playhouse.

Almost forgot. *Suffer* is on this week's spelling list. For our sentence exercise I wrote the quotation from my bookmark. I hope Mr. Barker is impressed.

Tuesday, October 16

Mr. Barker, impressed? What was I thinking? He didn't like the Biblical quotation in my spelling exercise and made me do it over. "Use the word in a sentence of your *own,* Miss Blackburn, showing that you understand the meaning. There'll be no copying from books."

I suffered in silence and did what I was told. And this is what I wrote: *I suffered in silence and did what I was told.* He said that was more like it.

Junior Red Cross after school. Muriel, Eva and I went and rolled bandages. We must have rolled thousands by now and they're always asking for more. What will happen when there's no more cloth for bandages? Will they end the war? What if there's no more ammunition or rifles or bayonets or mines or bombs or food? What if there are no more soldiers? Then they'll *have* to end the war. But how would they decide who'd won? Rolling bandages always makes me wonder about things like that. The other girls chat away happily, but not gloomy Charlotte.

Edith was too excited to eat supper tonight because she's walking out with Charlie, the handsome soldier from Winnipeg. He's taking her to the Empire to see a Charlie Chaplin film. Ruth's got a face like a dry mackerel, she's that envious. Duncan and I could give her some advice about catching a boy, based on our observations, but then she'd know we've been spying. She's not allowed to go walking out anyway.

I wonder if Jane lost her appetite, the way Edith has, when she started walking out with Luke. We haven't seen her in a while, but she must be missing him something terrible.

Muriel told me that envy is one of the seven deadly sins. I wonder if Ruth knows that. I won't tell her, because I'm as guilty as she is. I'm right envious of Muriel. Why? Because she has so many relatives. Twenty-one Chisholms in Richmond alone! Grandparents, cousins, second cousins, aunts and uncles, three little brothers and one baby sister. Whenever she turns around she sees a relative. If her brothers and sisters are driving her to distraction, she can go off to her grandparents' house and stay as long as she likes.

I wish we had dozens of relatives. I said that to Mum tonight, when we were doing the dishes, and she gave me one of her confusing looks, her eyes hurt and angry at the same time, and her mouth a thin tight line. The look that says, "The subject is closed."

One more thing. Dad must have overheard what I was saying about relatives, because just before I came upstairs he said, "Remember, Charlotte. What we lack in quantity, we make up in quality."

A nice thought to take to sleep.

Wednesday, October 17

Deirdre came back today. At recess Eva and I told her we were sorry about her brother. She thanked me, but then she looked Eva straight in the eye and said, "Why would *you* be sorry?"

Poor Eva. It's not the first time someone's said

something mean because her father's a German.

Got a C on my "Symphony of Autumn" and a new collection of Mr. Barker's red-pencil comments. *Incomplete sentence! Run-on sentence! No topic sentence! No concluding sentence! Sentence structure needs improvement!* And to cap it all off? *Too Wordy!*

Too Wordy!? What else would a written composition be but wordy? When we're doing our sums does Mr. Barker write *Too Numbery!*?

Duncan got a B on his composition. His sentences are perfect: *The leaves turn red. The wind blows them off the trees. I rake them into piles and jump in them. Autumn is fun!*

Well where's the symphony in that?

I read my composition after supper and everyone but Ruth said I deserved an A.

I know my sentences need improvement. It's because my mind moves faster than my hand and I'm in such a rush to keep up with my thoughts I forget all the little things like rambling sentences. But I hate the way Mr. Barker attacks my compositions with his bayonet pencil, so I'm determined to improve.

Mum says I should use my diary for practice and write each sentence as if Mr. Barker were going to read it.

Mr. Barker read my diary? Never! Not even in

my imagination! It would destroy the pleasure of writing altogether.

"Just do what Mr. Barker wants," Duncan said. "He obviously doesn't appreciate fine literature."

Fine literature! Hope I'll be able to sleep now that my head's swollen to twice its normal size.

Thursday, October 18

Don't know why, but the *Titanic* was on my mind this morning, so I asked Haggarty if he remembered when she went down.

"'Course I do!" he says. "It was only five years ago!"

He told me about the hundreds of bodies that were brought to Halifax by rescue boats, and how the mortuary workers had to label the possessions so that relatives could identify the victims. "Halifax had never seen anything like it," he said.

And today after school — oh, that Ruth! Now doesn't she want to go to Hollywood and be the next Mary Pickford. I came home early and caught her playing Mary Pickford in front of our vanity mirror. Her hands were over her heart and she was gazing up at the picture of Douglas Fairbanks, saying, "Oh, darling! precious love!" Mushy stuff like that.

"You won't think it's funny when I'm a star!"

she said when she caught me giggling.

Well she does have blond curls and dimples like Mary Pickford, but that's as far as it goes.

Oh, and a treat! The stores are allowed to sell canned veg again, so Mum sent me to Heine's to buy some peas and carrots. Eva and Werner were in the store helping their dad stock the shelves. I helped for a while, too, and Mr. Heine gave me a handful of penny candy. One of his handfuls, not mine, so I had lots to share when I got home. Except for that, and the "Mary Pickford" performance, it was an ordinary day.

Friday, October 19

Told Muriel how much I envied her, and she said she envied me! Why? Because I have a twin!

She asked what it was like to have a twin and I was stumped. No one's asked me that before. I can't imagine what it's like *not* to have a twin.

Well I thought for a bit, then told her that having a twin is like having a best friend, only better. At least that's how it is with Duncan and me.

Piano as usual. Kirsty waited outside while I had my lesson, but her friend with the treats wasn't there today.

Saturday, October 20

Why can't Ruth leave me alone? All I did was ask Duncan to wait for me, and Ruth says, "Have you ever thought Duncan might not want you tagging along?"

Well I hadn't thought, and I worried about it all the way to the harbour. Duncan finally told me to stop being silly. If he didn't want me to come along he'd tell me himself.

Saw hundreds of fellows in khaki and blue, as usual. A person can't take two steps around Halifax without tripping over a soldier or a sailor. Whenever I see a soldier I wonder if he'll end up wearing something I've knitted. I hope my socks won't fit too tight, or start to unravel before they even get to France.

Seemed like more ships than ever were in port today. The piers, the basin, every part of the harbour was packed. We saw an ocean liner, over twenty sailing ships, some oil tankers and some other ones. And big fighting ships like the *Highflyer*. The Germans better not try to attack us!

I bet we've seen ships from all over the world — the United States, Holland, Norway, Sweden, France, England and Denmark, as well as Canada. The ones from neutral countries like Norway have their name and country painted on the sides in huge letters, so other ships will know they're not the enemy. I like the troop ships the best because they're painted in "dazzle" patterns, with stripes and zig-zags and triangles. The *Olympic* is painted like that. Duncan says it's to confuse the enemy so submarines can't get a clear target. The ships probably look even more confusing when they're moving across the ocean.

I never paid much attention to ships before. Now I'm paying more attention, so when Luke comes home and reads my diary, he'll know what Halifax was like when he was away — even busier than it was when he left. Dad says it's sure not the sleepy old town it used to be.

Sunday, October 21

It's early morning. Ruth's snoring woke me up and drove me out of the bedroom, so I'm downstairs writing at the kitchen table. Dad's the only other person who's up. He's lit the stove and boiled the kettle, and now he's having a mug of tea and reading the newspaper.

He said I could let Kirsty in, a rare treat for Kirsty this time of year. She's sleeping at my feet. Good dog.

Muriel's question about twins has been on my mind because there's so much more I could have told her. For instance, Duncan and I can sometimes tell what the other is thinking. One of us will say something and the other will say, "I was just about to say that!"

Sometimes we finish each other's sentences, or start to hum the same tune at the same time.

If one of us is having a bad dream, the other will wake up and feel afraid, without even knowing what the dream was about.

Duncan knows when I'm worried without my saying a word. I can tell when he's worried, too, though that's a rare enough event.

Mum says we're "connected in a way that goes beyond understanding."

Now I hear someone moving around upstairs. Time to put my diary away.

Later

Edith's beau, Charlie, came for tea and gave everyone some Juicy Fruit gum. He looked right surprised when we all sang out, "The password to pleasure!" so Edith had to explain about Dad and his habit of quoting the newspaper ads and reciting poems. Duncan told Charlie we were having Solomon Gundy for tea and oh, the expression on Charlie's face! You'd think we were stewing up a neighbour. When he saw that Solomon Gundy was pickled herring and onions served with sour cream, he looked even more horrified. But he was game enough to try a bite and liked it well enough to try another.

"Good lad," says Mum. "Eat up while you can."

I hope Charlie and Edith get married after the war and move to Winnipeg. Then I could take the train out west to visit. I've never been farther west than Peggy's Cove, and that's but a crow's hop away.

Who was Peggy? What did she do to have a cove named after her?

Oh! Maybe she threw herself into the cove because her true love drowned at sea. No, what if that was only a rumour? What if he survived and came back for Peggy? But alas, he was too late! So he hurled himself off the top of the lighthouse and now their spirits are together.

I'd love to have a place named after me. Charlotte's Cove sounds nice, but I'd never drown myself to get the name.

There's a Charlottetown on Prince Edward Island, but it's named after a different Charlotte, so it doesn't count.

Monday, October 22

Miserable weather, and me in a growly mood all day.

Watched the cadets after school, Duncan and the others marching backwards and forwards and doing their rifle exercises. Duncan's not much taller than his rifle, they're that long.

Left after a while because I kept having visions of Duncan charging across No Man's Land and tripping over his rifle and being trampled in the mud. If they run out of soldiers will they lower the age to fifteen? Or even thirteen?

I asked Mum when I got home and she shouted at me. "Stop! Enough of your endless worries! Go and do something useful!"

She was in a growly mood, too.

And an hour ago, when Dad was coming home from a meeting, he spotted a light in my window. Didn't I get the scolding! "There's a reason for blackout curtains! If German planes were flying overhead they could see the light and drop their bombs! If the police had seen your light we could have been fined or gone to jail! It's dangerous!" And so on and so on.

I know, I know, I'm sorry — but it's not just *my* bedroom! It's Ruth's and Edith's, too, and they should've been scolded as well.

I didn't say anything, though. Just held my tongue and adjusted the curtains.

Oh, gosh, I'm tired of the blackout. It used to be fun walking up Fort Needham on a clear night and looking down at the lights. The cheery lights of houses, street lights guiding people here and there, lights in the shop windows, the twinkling lights of the harbour ferry, the lights of Dartmouth across the way. At least no one can black out the star lights.

How far away are the stars? What makes them twinkle? How I wonder what they are.

Tuesday, October 23

Went to Junior Red Cross with Eva and Muriel. Deirdre went, too, but this time she sat with some other girls. We heard them whispering behind our backs, saying mean things about Eva's dad being a German spy. We ignored them, but it was upsetting all the same. Especially since it isn't true. Because how could Mr. Heine be a spy? He's much too nice.

Muriel was upset because her favourite cousin, Todd, turned twenty last Saturday and there's a new law that says he *has* to join the army and fight in France. He never wanted to go in the first place, but now he doesn't have a choice.

Muriel said her dad told Todd he could start acting like more of an idiot than usual, since idiots can't be drafted.

I mentioned this at suppertime, and Dad said the real idiots are the ones running the war.

Mum gave him a look, but didn't he go on! Said the law wouldn't be "enforced" until after the election, but Prime Minister Borden would certainly be getting *his* vote because it was high time the government did something about men shirking their duty, and he was all in favour of "conscription," and shame on Todd for not volunteering in the first place.

Now I'm worried. What if Dad's right? What if Luke's fate is in the hands of an idiot?

Time for prayers and bed.

Wednesday, October 24

Nothing happened worth recording, so I'll muse.

Everyone says that Duncan and I are like night and day. Duncan's the day, quick with a smile and a cheery word. He's the sunny "burn" of Blackburn, whereas I'm "black" like the night. Dark and brooding.

Charlotte's a deep one, says Mum. Carries the weight of the world on her shoulders. Worry lines already. No wonder she's thin.

I don't mind that Duncan and I are different. At least we have the same dark hair and blue eyes. And besides, night and day are still part of the same twenty-four hours.

Thursday, October 25

Milk run this morning. I told Haggarty that sometimes I pretend he's my grandfather.

"I'm right proud to hear it," he said, and gave me a big hug.

I wonder what my real grandparents were like. I wish they *all* hadn't died early, before Mum and Dad even got married. Dad's mum died of pneumonia when he was ten, so he hardly knew her, and his dad and older brother died in a storm off Yarmouth a few years after that. Dad says he's probably got some relatives in Scotland, but good luck finding them. His parents had lost contact a long time ago.

When I asked Dad about Mum's parents — since *she* never says anything — he told me to "let sleeping dogs lie."

Friday, October 26

Weather mild and clear.

There's an exhibition of War Trophies in town and Mr. Barker told us it was our patriotic duty to go because it would give us a better understanding of the war if we saw things first-hand and asked questions. How can I have a *better* understanding when I don't understand it at all? Except that the Germans are shooting and gassing and blowing up our boys and it's all the Kaiser's fault.

My only question is the same as everyone else's: When will the war be over? People say it will be over soon, but they've been saying that since it started and that was three years ago.

But since it's my patriotic duty to go to the exhibition, I'll go in good spirits. And also because next week's composition will probably be "War Trophies" or something like that.

Eva said she'll go with me, even though she usually helps out in the store on Saturdays.

Piano lesson. Ouch, sore knuckles. Miss Tebo in a grumpy mood.

Saturday, October 27

A terrible day. After lunch everyone went off to the exhibition except for Ruth and me because I was waiting for Eva, and Ruth was looking for her locket. Well doesn't she go and accuse me of taking it. Right to my face she yells, "Tell me where you put it, I know you took it," and on and on until I finally snapped, "Stop blaming me! Blame the Kaiser!"

That really set her off. Before I knew it, she'd pushed me into the bedroom closet and locked the door. I screamed at her to let me out, but she wouldn't, just ran down the stairs and away outside, slamming the door behind her.

It came rushing back, all the other times she's locked me in the closet — the darkness, the panic, the fear of being trapped inside for hours. After a while I heard Eva downstairs, calling my name. I cried out that I was in the closet and up she came to my rescue. Ruth always leaves the key in the lock, but what good does that do me? Thank goodness for Eva.

But oh, the humiliation. Here I am, twelve years old, and Ruth can still make me cry and wet myself like a baby.

Edith once told me that Ruth was upset when I was born because she was used to being the youngest and getting all the attention. But isn't Duncan the youngest, too, not counting the nine minutes? Ruth is never mean to Duncan, probably because he's a boy.

Well, enough of Ruth.

Now for the exhibition. The war trophies were taken from the Germans by Nova Scotian soldiers and brought to Halifax. In addition to the trophies, like guns and such, there was a display of field hospital equipment with real nurses and orderlies on hand to answer questions. One of the orderlies was Charlie. I asked him if Edith had been to the display yet (she had), but I couldn't think of an intelligent medical question.

They also put on a demonstration that shows what happens to a wounded soldier, from the time he's brought into the field hospital by a stretcher-bearer to the time he leaves for the base hospital. I'd never thought of stretcher-bearers before. What a brave lot they are, tearing into No Man's Land to carry off the wounded.

After that we went to look at the German rifle that was captured by the Canadians at Vimy Ridge. I was telling Eva about Luke fighting at Vimy when some big boys from our school came over and told her that "Krauts" weren't allowed at the exhibition and she'd better get out before she was thrown out.

To my everlasting shame, I turned to go.

But Eva! She glares up at the boys and says, "I was born in Halifax, my mother was born in Halifax, and my father's a Canadian citizen. So I'm no more of a Kraut than you are." Those were her exact words.

The boys looked right stunned to see a girl standing up to them. They recovered quick enough, though, and muttered a couple of threats before backing off.

On the way home I told Eva I was sorry I hadn't helped her out, especially after she'd rescued me from the closet. She shrugged and told me she's had lots of practice standing up for herself. Most of the time she just ignores the name-calling.

"But it must hurt your feelings," I said.

"No," she said. "Because none of what they say is true."

I told her how much I admired her and how lucky I was to have her for a friend.

I still feel miserable, though. Duncan would have stood up for Eva, told the boys that she was as patriotic as they were, probably moreso, because how many socks had *they* knitted for our soldiers? How many bandages had *they* rolled?

That's what I *should* have said.

I felt sick to my stomach after seeing the war trophies and thinking of Luke being shot and carried out on a stretcher in a storm of bullets. I threw up after supper and Mum said I'm not to go to exhibitions like that, it only upsets me, and Mr.

Barker should have had more sense than to tell our class it was our duty to go. (The part about Mr. B. I heard her say privately to Dad.)

I was sick because of the bullies, too. Including Ruth, for locking me in the closet. I didn't dare tell, because Ruth would only make it worse the next time. Duncan says that Ruth picks on me because she can, and that I have to learn to fight back. Stand up to her, he says. Well I would, if I wasn't Charlotte the Meek.

If I wasn't Charlotte the Meek I could stand up to anybody.

What a miserable, cowardly day. Writing in my diary usually makes me feel better, but not tonight.

Sunday, October 28

Went to church and prayed that I'd be able to lock Ruth in the closet for once. Then I felt guilty and asked God to forgive me.

And wasn't I rewarded for my change of heart! For as we were leaving the church, Ruth told me she'd found her missing locket. Where? In the pocket of her Sunday coat, right where she'd left it last week. Being Ruth (and not Mary Pickford), she didn't think to apologize.

I was rewarded in another way, too. Because

when I was hanging up my Sunday dress, I saw the key and took it out of the keyhole. I'm going to throw it into the harbour. That way Ruth can never again lock me in, and I won't be tempted to do the same to her. I must be stupid as a bag of hammers not to have thought of *that* before.

After church, Charlie came for Sunday dinner.

Duncan and I dressed up in our Hallowe'en clothes and Charlie said he couldn't tell us apart until we smiled. He gave me some gum to cover up my crooked front teeth. The colour's not the same but no one will notice in the dark.

Ruth said she'd never guess we were twelve, the way we were carrying on.

Went over to Eva's in the afternoon, but she's come down with a cold. I hope she's better for Hallowe'en.

Monday, October 29

Mum spotted an ad in the newspaper for *Anne's House of Dreams* and told me I could start saving my pennies if I wanted it, which I do, even though it costs $1.50. I love the Anne books. Muriel does, too. Sometimes we pretend we're the characters in *Anne of Green Gables*. She's always Anne and I'm always Diana.

Today after school we acted out the scene

where Anne invites Diana to tea and gives her currant wine instead of raspberry cordial. Anne does most of the talking while Diana drinks the wine and gets drunk. Then she reels about dizzily and moans, "I'm awful sick. I must go home . . . "

We're going to practise and maybe put on a show for our families. Except Muriel can't invite all twenty-one Chisholms.

I'd rather be Anne than Diana, and have a more interesting part for once, but Muriel says I'm not spunky or outspoken enough. I have a "Diana personality," she says. Meek and sweet.

I told her I could *act* like Anne, but there's no persuading Muriel. Sometimes she's right bossy.

Clear and cool.

Tuesday, October 30

Went to see Eva after Junior Red Cross. She's still sick and can't go out for Hallowe'en.

Wednesday, October 31

Charlotte the Meek? Not tonight! We were on our way home when we saw two hooligans beating up Werner, not far from his dad's store. They were hitting and shoving, calling him "a dirty Kraut," and he was trying to get away.

Well Duncan charged right into the thick of it, yelling and swinging his sack at the bullies, and I did the same thing — without a second thought. It was a spunky Anne thing to do and not like me at all. Our sacks were heavy with apples so the bullies got a right good walloping, and didn't they go running off! It's more than apples that'll be wearing dark bruises tomorrow!

It had been stormy and cold all day, especially after dark, and Mum insisted we wear our combination underwear. We also had to tuck extra layers of newspaper in our coats to keep warm. It's a wonder we could *move,* let alone fly into the middle of a fight!

Well I gave Werner my handkerchief because his nose was bleeding and we walked to his house and had cocoa and gingerbread cookies with him and Eva. She's feeling a bit better.

When Mrs. Heine brought out the cocoa, Duncan and I said, "More food value than a cup of bouillon," just the way Dad does. We said it without thinking, at the exact same time, and everybody laughed.

It was fun trick-or-treating. The people whose houses we went to said pretty much the same thing. "If it isn't the Blackburn twins. Which is which?" Ha ha.

I'd swallowed the camouflage gum after the

first house, so as soon as we smiled we gave ourselves away.

Now it's all over, but I'm still worked up. My heart is racing and I have a sick feeling in my stomach. We didn't get a good look at the bullies, but what if they recognize Duncan and me at school or somewhere, and beat us up to get even?

Muriel's right. I am more of a Diana than an Anne.

Thursday, November 1

Milk run today.

Sometimes, between stops, Haggarty tells me stories. Tall tales from when he was a boy in Cape Breton and his grandfather rode whales and so on. Sometimes I tell *him* stories.

This morning I told him how Dad rescued Mum from a castle tower and whisked her away to safety.

"So that's how it was," Haggarty said. "Sure beats what I've heard."

What did he mean by that? I asked him to tell me, several times I asked, even begged, but he wouldn't budge. "Can't tell you," he said, "'cause it's not my story to tell."

I kept on. Was there a fire? Did the castle burn down? Is that what happened to Mum's parents?

Same thing. "Nope, can't tell."

I'll ask him again next week, but he can be right stubborn. Like the way he is with his first name. He won't tell *anyone* what it is. Even his own wife calls him Haggarty.

Next week I *must* remember my diary! Here it is November and I've still not shown him, even though I promised.

Later

We're making our own book! It's called *The Intrepidous Twins Fight the Forces of Dragon Man and Save the World from Evil.*

Duncan came up with the idea because of last night, the way we scared off the bullies. First we're going to think up the stories, then I'll write the words and Duncan will draw the pictures. Today we made the cover and pasted it on one of Edith's old scribblers.

Ruth said our title's too long and there's no such word as "intrepidous" and no such person as Dragon Man and the book is a stupid idea, but we just ignored her.

Duncan made up the name Dragon Man. He says Dragon Man has a long white beard and icy blue eyes. Sometimes he tricks you into thinking he's friendly and kind-hearted. You might stop for a chat. But watch out! His words will turn to flames and you'll be doomed forever, unless the Intrepidous Twins come to the rescue.

Dragon Man has control of all the Germans fighting in France, so sometimes the Intrepidous Twins have to go over there to help our boys. But most of the time they fight Evil at home. The twins' names are Charlotte the Fearless and Duncan the Brave, but no one knows their true identity. They sneak about the city, ever on the lookout for Dragon Man and his Minions.

If someone is struck by Dragon Man's piercing eyes or flaming tongue, their suffering is enormous — until the Intrepidous Twins take pity and rescue them.

But if they deserve to be punished, the Intrepidous Twins leave them in agony. So, wicked people, be warned! The Intrepidous Twins will show no mercy.

Friday, November 2

Today in Special Projects we started another knitting contest. This time, it's who will be first to finish a pair of socks on Number 10 needles. At least they're not Number 12s, but the 10s are bad enough. Why is it that the greater the number, the skinnier the needles? It should be the other way around. Anyway, we all sat together and cast on. Ready, set, GO! Off we went, our needles clicking like Kirsty's toenails on the kitchen floor.

Then Muriel started counting out loud. "Knit one, purl one, knit one, purl one."

Well it was right hard to concentrate, so I got even with, "Knit one, purl one, sit one, saint one."

Then Deirdre started in. "Fit one, furl one, fizzle one, faint one!"

Eva suggested we go right through the alphabet. We got all the way to *L* before Mr. Barker yelled at us to be quiet.

It was the best time I've ever had in knitting. Didn't drop a single stitch, but I got a terrible stitch in my side from laughing.

I did the rest of the alphabet by myself, on the way to my piano lesson. Here's my favourite: *Zit one, zurl one, zizzle one, zaint one.*

Saturday, November 3

Mum, Dad and Duncan went to the arena to see a moving picture called *Canadians Capture Vimy Ridge.* I wanted to see the film, too, since Luke and the 85th fought their first battle at Vimy, just this past April. But Mum said she didn't want me sick and upset the way I was after the War Trophies Exhibition.

It was a clear day and not too windy, so I took Kirsty for a long walk up to Fort Needham, then down to Haggarty's farm to see the new puppies. They look like small versions of Kirsty, white with chestnut-coloured patches. Kirsty was happy to see her mother and went bounding over yapping, "Come play with me!" but Princess was more interested in her new litter. Poor Kirsty.

The puppies are almost a month old. I wish I could have one, but Haggarty says they're all spoken for. Maybe when Princess has another litter, and if it's all right with Mum and Dad. It won't be all right with Kirsty, though! She's right spoiled.

Oh. The way Ruth was, I guess, before I came along.

Later

Duncan didn't see Luke in the film, or anyone else he recognized, and neither did Mum or Dad. They said that other people did, though, and there was no end of letting everyone know it with shouts of "Look, there's so and so from Dartmouth!" or Peggy's Cove and so on.

Mum wishes she hadn't gone. She's angry at the way Luke's battalion was sent in to capture an important position at Vimy, seeing as how the boys hadn't had any experience in battle. It was only because the other troops were doing badly, and the N.S. Highlanders were the last resort. Yes, she says, they surprised the Germans all right, and they took Hill Something-or-Other, and yes, it was a great victory for Canada, but the loss of life was staggering and it was a miracle that Luke survived. It was quite the speech for Mum and when she was finished she said she should have gone to Haggarty's farm with me.

Luke's battalion has a reputation now. They're called the "Never Fails." I hate that name. It's sure to bring bad luck, tempting fate that way.

Sunday, November 4

Church.

Duncan and I started a Table of Contents for our book. We were talking out our ideas when Duncan suddenly frowned and went quiet. I asked what was bothering him and he said he'd remembered something. Right out of the blue, he remembered seeing Dragon Man — not the character in his drawing, but a real live *person.*

It was at the Public Gardens, Duncan said, and he was about three years old. He was playing with a group of children, and there were a lot of people in the gardens, but he remembers the man clearly. Not only because of his white beard, and the silver dragon on his walking stick, but also because of something that happened between the man and Mum. Whatever it was, it frightened Duncan and made Mum cry.

Well we talked about that for a while, but Duncan couldn't remember anything more, so we went back to our chapters. Chapter One is called *The Intrepidous Twins Face Gaping Red Gullets of Guns!* Duncan's idea.

Chapter Two is *Charlotte the Brave Rescues Tenacious Troops from the Claws of Dragon Man!* My idea.

So far we've got ten chapter titles. Tomorrow we'll start on the stories.

Monday, November 5

Snow was falling this morning, but it turned to cold rain by noon and there was a biting northeast wind. Torture to walk home, the wind so strong. Dad said the longshoremen couldn't unload the ships at the dock.

Felt sick all day, especially in school with half the class coughing and sneezing.

Came home and worked on our book. Too cold for the playhouse so we worked in Duncan's room. Now that Luke's gone, Duncan the Lucky has the whole room to himself.

At least I have a bed to myself and don't have to sleep with Ruth. Parts of her may have "filled out nicely," but her elbows are right bony.

Almost forgot. Muriel's cousin Todd went hunting yesterday and shot himself in the foot. Now he won't have to get drafted. He said it was an accident, but nobody believes him. Muriel said he's safe on two counts now — "for being a cripple as well as an idiot."

The way she was talking, with a bit of a laugh and sounding right proud of her cousin — while brave people like Luke are going off and doing all the fighting — well it made me so mad I said, "Todd's nothing but a coward."

Well didn't she jump on me. She said that Todd's the smart one, that the boys over there are being "slaughtered for no good reason" and she knows a lot more about the war than I do and on and on till I was close to tears.

I wanted to argue back, I wanted to shake her, but the words jammed up in my throat. So much for trying to be Charlotte the Not-So-Meek. It's hopeless. I get so worked up with feelings, I lose my voice. Now I'm worked up all over again and won't be able to sleep.

At least we're still friends. Muriel agreed not to mention her cousin again, and I said I was sorry I called him a coward. (Even though I'm not.)

Friday, November 9

It's mid-morning, and I've been in bed with a cold since Monday night. The bedroom reeks of mustard, but the days of agony are over. No more falling asleep feeling like I'm Joan of Arc at the stake, no more waking up at midnight feeling that I'm buried in the cold, damp earth of a grave. A fitting composition topic for this time of year? "The Dirge of a Mustard Plaster Victim" . . .

Oh, no. Luke, when you're reading this, I'm sorry. I've just realized it's mustard gas the Germans are using over there.

Duncan caught the same cold as me and he's through with mustard plasters, too. Not Ruth, though. She came down with the cold yesterday (my fault, of course) and she's still being treated. She's asleep right now and our bedroom is nice and quiet, except for her wheezing.

Nothing much to write about. Yesterday Haggarty gave Mum a cup of cream, just for me. I shared it with Duncan. At noon Mum will bring up some beef bouillon, but I'd rather have cocoa. In the meantime I'm going to finish reading *Anne of Green Gables* for the second time.

Monday, November 12

Got up for a few hours today and did something mean.

Mum was busy with the wash, so she asked me to mix up some mustard paste and spread it on a piece of flannel for Ruth.

Now, Ruth thought it a fine joke when I was being plastered with burning flannel, so I secretly put in two extra spoonfuls of powdered mustard and smeared it on right thick.

Well, up Mum goes to the patient's bedside and onto Ruth's chest goes the plaster. Oh, the wailing! Dad must have heard it from the dry dock.

At first I didn't feel sorry, because the extra mustard won't kill her, and who knows? It might cure her more quickly.

But now I feel miserable. I don't think I've ever been deliberately mean, and even though my mind thought it was a good idea, it doesn't sit well inside.

I told Ruth I'm sorry, but I don't think she heard me. Mum gave her some syrup and she's sound asleep.

"Sorry, Ruth." There, I've said it again.

Tuesday, November 13

A letter from Luke!

He wrote it on October 21 near a place called Wipers. He didn't tell us the name, but we figured it out because he says he's "surrounded by gripers."

The town isn't really called Wipers, and as usual Mum was quick to point it out. "Ypres!" she said, pretending to sound annoyed. "Why doesn't that boy learn some French?"

We laughed and cried at that because it's such a relief to hear from him. Sometimes the mail can take six weeks to get here. Sometimes it doesn't make it at all because of the German submarines. Except Dad says the submarines haven't been such a problem since the ships started travelling in convoys, with battleships leading the way.

Luke, when you're reading this, I'm copying some of your letter in my diary, so you can skip the next part.

Thanks a million for the package. The smokes and letters and all. Gee I miss you folks. What wouldn't I give for some of Mum's roast goose and pumpkin pie!

Charlotte and Duncan, are you still giving Kirsty plenty of exercise? Give her a scratch behind the ears for me, will you?

Say, Kirsty, make sure those twins get a good

run, too. Don't want any lagging behind when I get home, not on the Blackburn Brigade.

The letter came at a good time. I was feeling that low about being stuck at home with a cold, but shame on me. It's not the trenches.

Thursday, November 15

Milk run today. Queenie gave a happy little whinny when she saw me, and Haggarty said he'd missed my company last week.

After the milk run I went back to school.

Ten in our class are away with whooping cough, including Carl, and a few others are home with colds.

We have a class project — filling a Christmas stocking. The Red Cross is collecting thousands of stockings from all over Canada and sending them to the wounded Canadians who have to spend Christmas in hospitals in England and France. Halifax has to contribute 1000. The stocking is huge but we can do it. Duncan and I went out right after supper and collected a few things from our neighbours. Little things like candies, cigarettes, a comb and bars of soap.

Just remembered a story Luke mentioned in a letter last year. He heard it from a British soldier.

It happened on Christmas Eve in 1914, the first Christmas of the war, when some German troops lit candles on little Christmas trees, and the British and French and Belgian troops started singing carols. The front lines were so close, the Germans heard them singing "Silent Night" and joined in. They sang other carols, too, all in their own language. Then something wonderful happened. They threw down their weapons and came together in No Man's Land. It was a Christmas miracle.

Luke told the British soldier it sounded like a fairy tale, but the soldier swore it was true. The troops even ate and drank together, and some of them exchanged addresses. They must have thought that the war would soon be over.

Here's the sad part. The generals got mad and ordered the troops to start shooting again.

How did I get started on that? Oh, the Christmas stockings.

After school Muriel and Eva and I were talking about the stockings and our knitting and Muriel says, "What did we do before the war?"

Well we were right stumped. There was a full moment of silence while we tried to remember, and then Eva said, "We must have learned how to knit."

It seems like such a long time ago.

At recess I told Eva and Muriel the story about the Christmas miracle.

Muriel didn't believe it, the know-it-all. She said, "The Huns kill babies with their bayonets. I hardly think they'd know our Christmas carols, let alone sing them."

Eva said her dad knows "Silent Night" and taught her the words in German, and would Muriel like to hear it? And on went the argument.

Well weren't they both surprised when I broke in and told them that the original words to "Silent Night" were written in the German language and that the English learned the carol from the Germans. Thank goodness for my Christmas carol piano book.

We couldn't have Special Projects this afternoon because of a special assembly in the auditorium. The whole school was there, and the teachers explained that everyone in Canada is responsible for helping our soldiers, even school children. How? By telling our parents to buy a Victory Bond.

Mr. Barker was even more dramatic than he was last year. "We must help crush the Hun with our money! Smash through to Victory! Buy Victory Bonds!"

I've got $1.00 saved up. I wanted to have $1.50 so I could buy *Anne's House of Dreams,* but I'm giving my dollar to Dad to put towards a Victory Bond so the government can buy rifles. Because what if Luke got wounded for lack of a rifle, because someone at home was too selfish to buy a Victory Bond? I'd hate that selfish person to be me.

Piano lesson, as usual. Now there's a boy who has his lesson after mine. The nice girl must have stopped taking lessons or changed her time. Too bad for Kirsty.

Saturday, November 17

Went to town with Duncan to buy winter stockings and who's on the trolley but Jane! We were some surprised, especially since she wasn't riding as a passenger but as the *conductor.* It's the first time we've seen a girl working on a trolley. Jane told us she'd got a letter from Luke last Monday (the day before we got ours), and Duncan the Bold says, "Was it a nice one? With *X*s and *O*s?"

Jane turned such a desperate red we didn't need an answer.

Then she took the letter out of her uniform pocket and showed us how Luke had taken a French stamp and put it on at an angle. We didn't know why *that* would make her happy, until she told us that it means "I love you!"

The trolley smelled of damp wool because of the rain, and the windows were all steamed up. We drew a heart on our window and wrote *Luke Loves Jane.* Jane threatened to throw us off when she saw it, but it was only her voice that was angry. Her face looked right pleased. After that we moved to another window and played tic-tac-toe. Jane gave us some toffees.

Now I've got some new things to wonder about.

What will Luke think when he finds out his sweetheart is working on a trolley?

I asked Mum and she said it's only until the war ends. Then the soldiers will get their old jobs back.

But what if Jane likes her job and doesn't want to give it up? Can they make her? And what if the war doesn't end? Could *I* get a job on a trolley?

Well Mum lost her patience, the way she does these days, and said, "Enough, Charlotte! Get those old flannel sheets if you've nothing better to do and start ripping!"

I wasn't fast enough to think of anything better to do, so I ripped up the flannel. Now it's ready for mustard plasters the next time somebody has a cold.

When I was finished, I said to Mum, "Cold comfort, that's a mustard plaster."

She told me not to be smart.

Then Ruth, playing the role of Mary Pickford, Suffering Patient, limped into the kitchen for a chat and I came upstairs to write in my diary. It's a treat having the room to myself.

Sunday, November 18

Got another bookmark today for reciting the 23rd Psalm. *The Lord is my shepherd* and so on. I love the part that goes, *He leadeth me beside the still waters.*

Still waters, there's a rare event in Halifax, but a beautiful phrase.

Muriel called me a show-off for memorizing things when I don't have to, but I wasn't showing off. I like to learn things by heart. It runs in the family. Dad can recite all sorts of poems, even long ones by Robert Service, like "The Shooting of Dan McGrew" and "The Cremation of Sam McGee."

Right now Robert Service is in France, driving an ambulance for the Red Cross. He wrote a book of poems called *Rhymes of a Red Cross Man.* Dad brought it home from the library. He was going to memorize a poem called "Fleurette," about a soldier who loses his leg and has terrible scars on his face, but we told him to find something more cheerful.

Ruth is over her cold and back to school tomorrow.

Monday, November 19

A Cloud of Doom has settled over our house and it's all because of me. Somehow I let it slip that Duncan and I saw Ruth down at the harbour a few weeks ago, flirting with sailors. So for the rest of November she's not allowed to leave the house on Saturdays and she has to come straight home after school.

Oh, she's some angry. After supper she did her chores and her schoolwork, then plunked herself down in the living room with her knitting. It was far from peaceful with Ruth snarling at the knits and purls and yanking at the wool as if she wanted to strangle someone. No need to guess who.

Pity the poor soldier who gets a pair of Ruth's socks in his Christmas stocking. They'll be so full of knots and bad humour, he'll want to fire them off at the Germans.

Secret Weapon unleashed by Canadian Forces! Halifax Socks take a Terrible Toll of Slaughter!

Good thing I threw away the key to the closet.

Later

Luke, when you're reading this, I'm sorry. I didn't mean to speak light of the war, about socks being a secret weapon.

Tuesday, November 20

My heart stopped when I came home from school and found Mum crying at the kitchen table. My only thought was that something had happened to Luke.

Thank heavens it wasn't that. It was a poem Mum cut out of the newspaper, and it's so beautiful and sad it made me cry, too.

It's called "In Flanders Fields" and I've already memorized the first verse:

In Flanders fields the poppies blow
Between the crosses, row on row,
That mark our place . . .

That's how it starts.

The poem was written by a Canadian doctor called John McCrae. He wrote it two years ago after seeing his best friend die on the battlefield in Flanders.

Today was the worst day of my life. At first it was special, because Mr. Barker had to leave the room and left me in charge of the class.

A few minutes later, Brian started singing, "Charlotte loves Carl," and half the class laughed and joined in.

Oh, the humiliation. I said it wasn't true but Brian said it was. And to prove it, he held up the secret note I'd put inside Carl's desk.

Well I tried to grab it but Brian jumped up and waved it out of my reach, still singing, "Charlotte loves Carl," so I started to chase him — and in walks Mr. Barker.

Instant silence. Brian and I stop dead in our tracks.

Mr. Barker doesn't ask what happened or who started it, just hauls us up to the front for the strap. "I never would have expected this of you, Miss Blackburn," he says, and gives me a stinging whack on each hand.

On the way back to my seat I caught Duncan's eye. I could see he was upset so I said, "It didn't hurt."

I said it softly, almost in a whisper, but Mr. Barker with the third ear, he heard me and said, "Then get back here for another one!"

Well, then I couldn't hold back the tears, and my hand was shaking so much he missed the first time, and didn't he make up for it, the hateful swine.

After school Muriel said she was surprised, the way I'd chased after Brian. "It's just what Anne would've done," she said, and her voice was full of admiration.

She told me that I could be Anne the next time we play a scene, but I'd rather be Diana after all.

Thursday, November 22

Wind, rain and snow. Mum wouldn't let me go on the milk run, in spite of my pleading.

"And have you catch your death in this weather? No!"

So Ruth pipes up, "What about catching our death on the way to school?"

The very thing I wanted to say, but only Ruth was brave enough to say it. Of course we had to go to school anyway.

After school Duncan and I wrote a new chapter in our book, in which Bully Barker gets captured by Dragon Man, and the Intrepidous Twins ignore his cries when he's getting strapped. Duncan the Fearless and Charlotte the Brave rescue him in the end, but only after he swears he'll never yell at his class or use the strap again. To make sure he keeps his promise, they chop his strap into little pieces and make him swallow every last one in front of the school at a Special Assembly. It takes a long time. And as they watch, the students of Richmond School clap their hands with glee.

Luke, when you're reading this, you might wonder why I wrote a note to Carl. It was to cheer him up when he comes back to school after having the whooping cough. It said, *Dear Carl, I hope you're feeling better. Yours truly, Charlotte.* I drew a few red hearts on the paper, but only for decoration, because they're easy to draw.

Bully Barker ripped up the note and threw it away. I'm not going to write another one, not with Brian Nosey Parker around. He had no business snooping in Carl's desk in the first place. Just wait until he's in the clutches of Dragon Man.

Friday, November 23

Edith is making me a velveteen dress for Christmas! It will have a white collar and cuffs and be shirred around the waist. The colour is called Midnight Blue.

I've never had a velveteen dress before.

Saturday, November 24

The Intrepidous Twins have uncovered a big secret.

Late this afternoon, when Duncan and I were coming back from Carl's house, we spotted Ruth talking to a group of her friends. We ducked behind a shed and listened, and after that we went over the words so we wouldn't forget.

" . . . last day I'm spending in school," Ruth says. "I've got a job at the telephone company."

"You have to be sixteen," says one of her friends.

"I'm close enough," says Ruth. "And what do they care? They're desperate for workers and they said I could start on December sixth."

Then Duncan and I had a dilemma. Should we tell on Ruth? We talked it over and finally decided not to. Ruth might be making it up to impress her friends, and if she isn't, well just let her try picking on me now! Duncan says a spy should always have a secret stashed away, because you never know when it might come in handy.

Carl's feeling better. We played Geography at his house but couldn't make any noise because of his Uncle Ted. He's staying at Carl's until he's well enough to go home to Amherst. He just came back from the war and has shell shock.

Every night he has nightmares and wakes up screaming. Whenever he hears a loud noise, like the trolley bell ringing or a door slamming shut, he drops to the floor and covers his head because he thinks the Germans are attacking.

Sunday, November 25

One month from today I'll be wearing my midnight blue velveteen dress. Edith says the colour's a perfect match for my eyes.

Duncan suggested we send our Dragon Man book to Luke for Christmas. Ruth overheard and said it was a stupid idea, which means it's a wonderful idea and she wishes she'd thought of it.

We're going to write one more chapter. It's called, *The Intrepidous Twins (with the help of Luke the Courageous) Smash through to Victory! Dragon Man is Vanquished! Peace Rules the World!*

Monday, November 26

Went to the store for Mum after school and Mr. Heine gave me his usual handful of candy. I'm glad Mum still shops at Heine's store. Muriel's mum hasn't gone there since the beginning of the war. I don't understand, since Mr. Heine is the same person he was before. At least

Muriel's still allowed to play with Eva.

I wonder what will happen when the war ends. Will his old customers go back as if nothing has happened?

One week left in the sock-knitting contest, but I have no hope of winning. Eva's finished six pairs to my four. A lady in the South End has knitted 193 pairs of socks since the war began.

I put my best socks in our family's Christmas package for Luke. All the other pairs are going to the Red Cross. I finished the balaclava, but it's twice the size of a normal head.

Just had a terrible thought. What if we don't win the war?

I wouldn't dare say that out loud.

Tuesday, November 27

Weather sunny and cold.

Edith mailed our Christmas package to Luke today. Where will he spend Christmas this year? Last year he wrote and told us how the soldiers gathered in a deserted building behind enemy lines and sat down for a Christmas dinner. After dinner they received all the Christmas boxes and stockings that were sent from home.

We didn't finish our book in time to send it. Lucky for Luke, says Ruth.

Wednesday, November 28

Mum looked me over today and said, *Quelle surprise!*

The surprise? I've grown taller (not wider) without even noticing. Now I can wear Ruth's hand-me-down dresses, once Mum takes in the seams. Two of me could fit into Ruth's dresses now. The dark green and white check is my favourite.

Poor old Billy the Pig. His goose is cooked, his days are numbered, and so on. He doesn't know it, though, so at least his remaining days won't be ruined.

I asked Mum what it would be like, going along from day to day with no worries and nothing to wonder about. She told me to put my mind to better use. So I came upstairs and wrote in my diary. Now what? Guess I'll practise my arpeggios. They're harder to play than scales, but I love the way the notes skip under my fingers.

Weather cold, with light snow falling.

Thursday, November 29

This morning I gave Haggarty my balaclava and said Queenie could have it to keep her ears warm. But Haggarty? He puts it on over his hat and says he'll wear it himself!

He looked right silly, with one of the eye holes big enough for his entire face. Every stop we made, people laughed. I'm glad my balaclava's good for something.

And socks! The first pair I knitted on those skinny Number 10s are all out of shape and I'm too embarrassed to send them to the troops. Dad said the boys wouldn't mind so long as the socks were warm, but if I really don't want to send them, I could give them to him. So I did.

"A perfect fit for my big feet!" he says.

Not true, but kind of him to say so.

Friday, November 30

Hurried home from school to try on my midnight blue velveteen dress. Edith had me stand on a chair in our bedroom so she could pin up the hem, but I kept fidgeting, I was that excited, because the dress, oh, it's beautiful!

Finally Edith lost her patience and said, "If you don't stop squirming, you'll never get the dress!"

It was the first time Edith's ever spoken to me like that and I was shocked into standing still.

"Edith!" said Ruth. "What's got you in such a snit? Sir Winnipeg not coming tonight?"

That's Ruth for you, always quick with the hurtful words.

Edith ignored her, but didn't I give Ruth a glare, the heartless beast. As if she could ever be like sweet Mary Pickford.

When Edith finished pinning the hem she apologized for losing her temper.

And Charlie DID come calling, like he's been doing at least twice a week. So ha ha on Ruth.

I wish we'd hear from Luke. "No news is good news," Mum says, but she says it to convince herself, I think, because her eyes can't hide the worry.

Maybe he's busy writing diary entries instead of letters. I hope so. I'd hate to think his life in the trenches is so wretched he can't bring himself to write in his usual good-humoured way.

He's hardly ever complained. Except when he was describing No Man's Land. Mum says she's grateful for that, and I am, too, because don't we already know from the returning soldiers how awful it is over there?

Muriel told me that her dad's cousin got "trench mouth," a horrible gum infection, and as soon as one person gets it, *everyone* gets it. Same with lice. She started to tell me about the rats that live on the dead soldiers' corpses, but I couldn't stomach any more and told her to stop.

Saturday, December 1

Duncan and I took Kirsty for a run on Fort Needham. We threw her ball and raced her for it, but she won every time. She's right lively for a seven-year-old dog.

Then Carl came along with Boots. Kirsty and Boots tore around greeting the other dogs on the hill, and Duncan and Carl and I had foot races.

It was some fun until Brian showed up and started teasing me. Then he tripped me, but ha ha on him, I caught myself in time and didn't fall.

After that a bunch of other kids joined us and we played Red Rover, boys against girls. I was always the first girl chosen, no thanks to Brian. Sometimes I had to hold his hand. Thank goodness we were wearing mittens.

Now why would Brian tease me and trip me, then choose me? I won't ask Edith, because she'll say what she said before, that boys often do silly things to get a girl's attention. Like Carl and my knitting. But Brian, sweet on me? I hope not!

Now that it's December, I wish it would snow. Can't wait to go coasting.

Sunday, December 2

Church this morning.

Practised the piano this afternoon. Ruth laughed whenever I hit a wrong note, but I ignored her and after a while she went away. Then Edith and I played duets.

Tomorrow's the first day of winter hours so school doesn't start until 9:30. I can sleep in! (But probably won't.)

Monday, December 3

Today we learned that a story has a beginning, a middle and an end. But what comes before the beginning? What comes after the end? Didn't dare ask Mr. Barker for fear of being called impudent, like the last time I asked a wondering question, but I asked the family at supper.

Ruth puts on a pious expression and says, "In the beginning God created the earth. World without end, Amen."

Mum gives an "Oh, Charlotte" sigh and says, "You'll be old before your time with all your wondering. *Carpe diem* is my advice. Seize the day."

Then everyone else added their two bits worth.

"Gather ye rosebuds while ye may," says Edith.

"A stitch in time saves nine," says Duncan.

"Make hay while the sun shines," says Dad.

We all laugh when Ruth points out, "That's what I want to do, but you never let me!"

My family, the philosophers. The mood was right cheerful, though no one really answered my question, and I'm still trying to figure out what Duncan's "stitch in time" has to do with any of the other sayings.

After I did the dishes I played the piano and Duncan played his harmonica and the music took my mind off things.

Now I wonder, Who created God?

What will happen to me in the end?

Tuesday, December 4

Luke's been seriously wounded. It happened on October 28th at the Battle at Passchendaele. That's in Flanders, where the "poppies blow."

We found out today, in a letter he wrote on November 14th, and we were all upset and in tears. Dad was furious that the army hadn't notified us way back when it happened, or listed Luke's name among the casualties in the newspaper.

Well it was a long letter, and after supper we sat in the living room and took turns reading it out loud, several times, and before long we realized that it's a good thing Luke was wounded, because now he's safe in a hospital, and in England, and well enough to write a letter.

He starts it *Dear Folks and Kirsty.*

As soon as she heard her name, Kirsty perked up her ears and listened. Smart dog!

Luke says the battle at Passchendaele was a "hellish nightmare" from start to finish. The attack began at dawn on October 26, and for three days the Never Fails and other battalions inched their way forward, fighting in cold mist and rain, plastered with mud, praying they wouldn't be "sucked into the swamps and left to die," but near dead anyway from exhaustion.

They reached higher and drier ground on the 28th, and that's when Luke was "caught in a barrage of artillery fire."

The stretcher-bearers managed to carry him out of No Man's Land, and a horse-drawn ambulance took him to an aid station for serious casualties. On November 1st he was evacuated to England.

A shell fractured his left thigh bone so his leg's in a cast, and the doctors weren't able to remove all the shrapnel. As if that weren't enough misery, he came down with "a touch of bronchitis."

On the good side, he hopes to be walking on crutches before long and won't be leaving the hospital until late December. And he's being cared for by "the best nursing sisters in the world."

At least he survived, and we thank God for that.

At the end of the letter, Luke asks us to keep him in our prayers, and of course we will — now more than ever. Because as Mum says, Luke has a way of putting a good face on everything, and his condition may be worse than he lets on.

Later in the evening, Charlie came to call. Mum let him read Luke's letter, and Charlie promised to visit Luke in hospital as soon as he gets to England.

"Is it only three days until you leave Halifax?" asks Ruth the Heartless, knowing full well the answer.

That got Edith and Mum crying all over again.

Wednesday, December 5

Well the house was ablaze with excitement this morning, because last night Charlie gave Edith an engagement ring. It's fit for a princess, with two little pearls and a sparkly blue stone. They're not getting married until after the war, and Mum and Dad say that's right sensible.

I walked with Edith on her way to work and listened to her wedding plans. Gosh, she must have been awake all night with the planning — the dress, the flowers, the way St. Mark's will be decorated and so on. She wants a June wedding, the first June after the war ends, and she wants Ruth and I to be her bridesmaids.

After the wedding she and Charlie are going to live in Winnipeg, and she said that Duncan and I could take the train and go for a visit. Now I have all the more reason to pray for the war to be over soon.

When she wasn't talking, Edith was weeping, one minute for joy and the next minute for sorrow, since Charlie's shipping out on Friday. I promised I'd pray for him as well as for Luke, and that made her happy. At least Charlie will be working in a hospital and not fighting on the front line.

I'll have lots to tell Haggarty tomorrow, what with Luke being wounded and Edith being engaged!

And I *must* remember to show him my diary, with Luke's cheerful letter on the first page. I'll write myself a note and put it beside my boots right now so I won't forget.

One more thing. Duncan reminded me that tomorrow's the day Ruth is planning to start working at the telephone company. We thought about telling Mum and Dad but decided to wait and see what happens. They're sure to find out anyway.

And one *more* thing. Late last night someone broke a window in Mr. Heine's store.

Thursday, December 6

Well it's seven in the morning and here I am, snuggled up in the comforter with the bedroom all to myself and no need to rush. I love winter hours.

The curtains are pulled back and the day is taking shape. There's a light frost on the ground, a haze of grey smoke drifting out of the chimneys and a mist rising off the harbour.

Dad's left for the dry dock. He was whistling as he went and I sang along in my head. *"What's the use of worrying, It never was worthwhile, So pack up your troubles in your old kit bag, And smile, smile, smile . . . "*

Edith's playing the Chopin waltz. Ruth's in the kitchen talking to Mum, and Duncan's outside getting more wood for the stove. He comes in, slams the door and drops the wood, so now Mum's scolding and Kirsty's barking at the fuss.

"Kirsty, how did you sneak in?" says Mum. "Duncan, put her outside!" More scolding.

"It's cold, Mum! Let her stay in!"

Nope. Poor Kirsty. Out she goes.

Now Edith and Ruth are saying goodbye. Mum the Detective asks Ruth why she's in such a hurry to get to school. Ruth says she has an essay to finish and wants to do it in the classroom where it's quiet.

I can picture her expression, Ruth acting the Diligent Student. Ha ha. Good thing I'm not downstairs. I'd probably start laughing and give away her secret.

Well, now things are quiet. Not a sound from Duncan — he must be eating his breakfast. I better get my porridge before he takes all the cream. Then it's time for the milk run and smile, smile, smile!

I'm in a hospital, in a corridor, sitting on the floor.

What happened? How did I get here?

The corridor is jammed with people. Some covered with blood and black grime. Some with faces that don't look like faces. Others rushing around, too busy to answer questions.

Someone is screaming but most of the people are quiet.

There's blood all over the floor. The smell . . .

How did I get here? I was outside with Haggarty. But what happened after that? Did I walk here? Did someone carry me? Who?

I remember seeing bodies. Bodies everywhere . . . and parts of bodies. Crushed and burned and mangled. And the sounds of shrieking and sobbing and moaning . . .

All I can remember thinking is, the Germans must have come. This must be No Man's Land.

People keep going past down the corridor. They're crying, calling out names, looking for friends or relatives.

Where's Dad? Why doesn't he come for me?

Some people are lying on stretchers, not moving. Soldiers are sorting through them, and saying, "This one's for Chebucto." What do they mean?

I have to keep writing to stay awake, or else they'll think I'm dead and take me away. Then no one will find me.

I must have fallen asleep, because it seems later in the day somehow.

I remember I was outside on Citadel Hill. How did I get there? And how long was I there? The town clock showed 9:05, but the hands never moved.

Oh, now I remember how I got here. A soldier brought me in a motor car — yes, that's it. He wrapped me in his greatcoat and I found my diary in one of the pockets. How did *it* get there? I found a pencil, too. It's sticky with blood.

I keep watching for Dad or Edith or Ruth. Where are they?

I don't want to remember any more.

I fell asleep again, and dreamed that we were all safe at home. But then I woke up.

I'm still in the nightmare of No Man's Land.

I'm in a ward now, and there are patients everywhere. They're lying in beds, on mattresses, on the floor between the beds. There are three little girls in the bed next to mine, but so far I'm the only one in my bed.

There's no glass in the windows, only blankets strung up to keep out the cold. Is it night?

The only light is from candles and oil lamps. The flames flicker and make nightmare shadows.

I'm cold and scared and I can't stop shaking. I wish Dad would come.

A nurse just came and cut off my hair. It was matted with blood and bits of glass. She cut off my clothing and washed me and gave me a nightgown.

She says I'm in Camp Hill Hospital. It's Thursday night, five after ten, thirteen hours since the burning ship exploded. Then she rushed off to another patient.

The burning ship . . . Yes, I remember, and then the explosion . . . Was it only this morning? How can it still be the *same* day?

The nurse said I'm a brave young lady but that I have to try and sleep.

I don't feel brave. I'm afraid of falling asleep and having the dream again. Because when I wake up . . . it's too hard.

I tried to tell the nurse that, but I can't seem to talk.

I have to keep writing. I promised Luke. He has to know what happened here.

But I can't write about the explosion. Not yet.

I hurt all over.

A doctor has put stitches in my foot and in my cheek, but I didn't scream.

Then another nurse came to bandage my other cuts — not the nurse who cut my hair, but a younger one. She told me her name was Helen and asked if I recognized her.

I didn't at first, not until she mentioned her piano lessons, and how they came after mine on Friday afternoons. Then I remembered. She used to bring treats for Kirsty. It seems like a hundred years ago.

A little girl is sharing my bed now. Her name is Violet. She's four. One of her eyes was removed. It was full of splinters.

Helen said that lots of people have been blinded. They were looking out their windows and when the explosion happened, showers of glass flew into their faces. She said I'm lucky that my eyes are all right.

I saw a headless body. Someone else with a face split in two. A boy with a rivet through his eye. A person on fire, still alive, hanging from a telephone wire.

Am I lucky to see such horror? I'd rather not see at all.

Violet is whimpering in her sleep. I'm afraid to go to sleep. I'm afraid to stay awake.

I think it's the middle of the night now. The wind is howling.

People keep coming in, quietly saying names, looking at faces. They have to look closely because so many faces are scarred, burned, covered with bandages.

Friday, December 7

It's early morning.

They say there's a heavy snowstorm. I can still hear the wind howling.

More of the wounded are brought in, and more people come looking. They bring the cold in with them and leave puddles of melting snow on the floor.

Will Dad come for me today? Will he recognize me? What if I'm sleeping when he comes, and I don't hear him calling my name? What if he doesn't notice me?

I have to keep writing.

I found out that Helen's a student at the university, not a nurse. She wants to become a doctor. That's why she stopped taking piano lessons. She was too busy studying. I didn't know a girl could be a doctor.

After the explosion, she set off to Victoria General Hospital to help out. But when she saw all the stretchers coming into this hospital she decided to stay here.

The nurses, the doctors, the volunteers — they never stop to rest, not even at night. There are too many wounded, hundreds and hundreds, and more coming in all the time.

Later

Helen stopped by for a second to give me back my diary. She took it away after breakfast and told me I had to get some sleep. I slept for three hours.

Helen said, "I'm sorry I took your diary. I know it gives you comfort," and kissed my cheek.

I wanted to cry but I couldn't.

The hurt is too big for tears.

Afternoon

Now there's a blizzard. Someone said it's the worst blizzard in years. I can't see outside because the windows are now covered with boards, but I can hear the wind and pelting snow. How will the rescuers find people now? And yesterday, in the snowstorm, what happened to the people still trapped inside buildings?

I've still got the soldier's greatcoat. It's keeping me warm, like an extra blanket.

A reporter is in the ward, asking everyone their names. He said that reporters are doing this in all the hospitals and shelters so that the newspapers can print the names of the survivors.

I managed to tell him my name, but when I said Charlotte Blackburn, it sounded as if it belonged to somebody else.

Saturday, December 8

Dad and Edith

Sunday, December 9

I don't want to write any more. But I have to try. My diary is the only anchor I have now. It might be all I have left of home.

Muriel's mother came yesterday and told me about Dad and Edith. She'd gone to the morgue at Chebucto like hundreds of others, looking for her husband and relatives, and when she saw my dad she identified him. She saw Edith, too, but her body had already been identified by someone. Mrs. Chisholm said that almost all the workers at the dry dock were killed. Like my dad and Muriel's dad.

Almost everyone who worked on the waterfront or close to the waterfront, like Edith did, was killed, either by the blast or by the tidal wave that came after.

The explosion sucked back the sea, and when the water rushed back in

Mrs. Chisholm asked about the rest of my family, but I couldn't speak. I don't know what happened to Ruth. But Mum and Duncan

I couldn't —

I can hardly bear to write their names.

Afternoon

I tried to eat a bit of soup, but couldn't. All I could do was sleep. When I woke up, Violet was gone — I don't know where. I'm afraid to ask.

Someone said it was bitter cold yesterday, with the blizzard and over a foot of snow, and anyone who was hurt but not found will have frozen to death.

Today there is rain, slush and flooding.

Three ladies from a relief committee have just been to see me. They're visiting all the children in the hospital. They gave me warm clothes, winter boots and a pair of slippers. They asked questions about my family, but all I could do was shake my head.

Later on a doctor looked at my stitches and said I can leave the hospital in a few days.

Then Mrs. Chisholm came again. She knows about Mum, now. She saw her name in the newspaper, in the list of "known dead." She brought me a newspaper, and we read through the list of "known survivors," hoping to find Ruth, but she wasn't there. Mrs. C. said she could still be alive, but missing, and that I mustn't give up hope.

We looked for Duncan's name, too, even though I knew it wouldn't be there, but praying that a miracle . . .

Mrs. Chisholm said I can stay at her house when I leave the hospital, that it would be good for Muriel to have a friend at home. Muriel wasn't badly hurt, but she's grieving something terrible for her dad.

Tomorrow there's a burial service for the Chisholms. Muriel's dad, two uncles, an aunt and six cousins, including Todd, who shot himself in the foot for nothing. All those relatives gone, and Mrs. Chisholm still has time to think of me.

Later

Sunday night and I haven't said one prayer. I don't think God is listening. Not to those of us who lived in Richmond.

Later, still Sunday

I said a prayer after all, for Luke. I may be the only one left who can.

Monday, December 10

Charlie came this morning. At first I was afraid he'd ask about Edith, and I'd have to be the one to tell him, but it turns out he's known from the start. It was one of his soldier friends who found her body and identified her. He had met Edith before and knew about her and Charlie's engagement.

Two days ago, after Charlie had seen the lists in the newspaper and knew for certain that I had survived but Mum and Dad hadn't, he sent a telegram to Luke, directly to the hospital where he's recovering. "Some of the telegraph lines were already up and running," he said. "It's the one thing I could do. Edith meant the world to me, and your family . . . " He tried to say more, but his voice kept breaking.

Charlie was supposed to leave Halifax on the 7th, but the medical corps stayed to help with the wounded. They're leaving tomorrow in a convoy of thirty-three ships, with *Highflyer* as escort.

Charlie promised again that he'll visit Luke in the hospital, once he arrives in England. He'll tell Luke that we don't know for certain about Duncan or Ruth. I didn't let on what I know about Duncan.

After Charlie left, I read the list of survivors more closely and found Haggarty. His first name is Ethelbert. No wonder he kept it a secret.

And then I saw Eva's name. Her parents and Werner are survivors, too.

I tried to read the names of the dead, but I only got as far as *Jane Best* and had to stop.

Poor Luke. I hope he doesn't find out about Jane, because how much hurt can he bear, especially in the middle of a war?

Jane's name came after Mr. Barker's.

No more compositions or red-pencil comments. *Too Wordy,* he used to say. It made me so mad. As if little things like that could matter.

What matters now is that I write about what happened on that horrible day, what I did, and what I know. I can't talk about it, but I have to write it down for Luke.

I'll assign myself a composition. I'll make myself remember, and I'll record every detail, from beginning to end.

So Luke, this composition is for you.

Charlotte's Composition: Thursday, December 6, 1917

It was a beautiful morning. I laced up my boots and put on my coat, and Mum

I can't do it.
I'll try again tomorrow.

Later

I put on the dressing gown the relief ladies gave me, and one of the slippers. The other one doesn't fit because of the bandage on my foot.

Helen helped me limp to the bathroom. My legs felt weak and shaky.

My foot still hurts, but this kind of pain is easier to bear than the other kind. There's not a minute goes by that I don't think of Duncan, and

Mum and Dad and Edith, even Ruth, but it's too hard to write . . .

I can't believe they're gone.

Tuesday, December 11

No matter how much it hurts to remember, I'm determined to write my account of the Explosion. Here it is.

Charlotte's Composition:
Thursday, December 6, 1917

On Thursday morning, December 6, I laced up my boots and put on my coat. The ground was white with frost. Mum told me to wear my warm hat. I remembered to take my diary to show Haggarty.

Kirsty was waiting in the front yard. We chased each other around until Haggarty came.

We went from stop to stop as usual. People came out for their milk as usual.

I showed Haggarty my diary between the stops, and read bits out loud. Like the part about Mum living in a castle and Dad coming to her rescue. I was begging Haggarty to tell me the true story, and he was making up one tall tale after the other. We were laughing, Kirsty was woofing hellos to anything that moved. Just like a regular Thursday.

Then we heard the clanging screech of metal against metal. People started rushing out of their houses. I remember Mrs. Reilly waving to us and shouting, "Never mind the milk you look to the Narrows a collision two ships!" All in one breath.

We looked to the harbour and saw the ships. *Imo,* with big letters saying BELGIAN RELIEF, and *Mont-Blanc. Mont-Blanc* was on fire and drifting close to the piers.

People from everywhere, throngs of people, were running down to the harbour for a better look, standing on the docks and on flat roofs like the one at the Acadia Sugar Refinery. I remember saying to Haggarty, "Lucky Dad, he'll have a right good view. So will Edith, from her office window."

We were mesmerized. The fire had only just started, but great clouds of steam and black smoke were already gushing into the air, and blue and orange flames were billowing way up to the sky.

I wanted to get Duncan, to make sure he didn't miss it. So I said goodbye to Haggarty, grabbed my diary and ran off towards home with Kirsty. I don't know exactly where I was when the explosion happened, because I was still keeping an eye on the fire. It was spectacular, like nothing you could ever imagine.

There was no warning for the explosion. It happened fast, and all at once.

The roar of the flames just stopped. I saw a white flash shoot up from the burning ship and felt a tremendous blast of air, a whirlwind that swept me up and hurled me around until it suddenly gave out and dropped me. I didn't know where I was, only that I'd come close to landing on a picket fence. Bodies were lying everywhere. Nothing moved, no one spoke. And then the screaming began.

I thought it was the end of the world.

I have to stop now. Volunteers are coming around with tomato soup. It must be almost noon.

Tuesday afternoon

A soldier brought me my soup. His name is Eddie. He has one arm. He and some other wounded soldiers were recovering here, but they had to make room for all the people hurt in the Explosion. The soldiers who can move about are helping the volunteers.

Eddie talked and made little jokes while I was eating my soup. He said he'd go back to France one day and look for his other arm.

After lunch I hobbled up and down the corridor using a cane.

There are lots of patients in worse shape than I am. I mean, worse on the outside. Eddie says that the wounds you *can't* see are often the worst.

The bandages are off my face. My cheek feels puffy. I don't know what it looks like because the mirrors were shattered like the windows.

Later

This morning, once I got started on my composition, it felt as if I were looking on from a far-away place, and writing about somebody else. Now I'm going to try and write a bit more.

Luke, when you're reading this, what happens next is the hardest part.

Charlotte's Composition, Part 2: Thursday, December 6, 1917

After the explosion, a horrible black, oily rain started to fall. It soaked through my dress, my underwear, my stockings and stuck to my skin like tar. My coat and hat were torn off by the blast and one of my boots was gone.

I stood up, scared and shaken to the heart, and tried to get my bearings. There was so much wreckage, and so many bodies, I had to watch every step. That's how I stumbled on my diary. I wasn't even surprised, just picked it up and kept going.

Nothing looked the same. I heard myself say out loud, "This must be No Man's Land."

Streets gone, trees uprooted, telegraph poles knocked down, wires tangled and shooting sparks, a trolley hurled from the tracks. Every house in ruins, and in some, flames leaping from the wreckage. Black smoke overhead and over the harbour.

My only thought was going home. Mum and Duncan were there and they'd know what to do, they'd keep me safe. But where was home? My whole neighbourhood, the whole of Richmond, was flattened.

It was hard to move through the rubble. Glass everywhere, and I cut my foot badly. I remember tripping over a dead dog and lurching out of the way of a panicking horse. I saw a man who'd lost every stitch of clothing, but I wasn't shocked to see him stark naked. All this time I was praying. *Our Father who art in heaven . . . Please, God, let this not be happening . . . Please, God, please let Mum be safe, let Duncan be safe . . .*

A storm of people, faces black from the rain and streaked with blood. People rushing to escape, to put out fires, rushing to help those who needed help, using boards or doors to carry away the injured, searching through the wreckage for survivors. People in shock, not moving at all. Others dead or dying. Ambulances, soldiers, all trying to get in past the frantic crowds that were desperate to get out.

Somehow I got home. Our house was mostly in ruins. One section was still standing; the rest was splintered wood, broken furniture, the stove overturned and coals spilling out, shards of jagged glass, clear glass, stained glass, the floor inches deep in glass and wood and plaster.

I stumbled through what had been the kitchen and found Mum. Buried but still breathing.

I remember saying, "Mum, I'm here, I'll get you out."

And she cried, "Ruth, is it Ruth? I can't see!"

I told her it was Charlotte, but I don't know if she heard me.

I tore at the wreckage, lifted and heaved with a strength that came from somewhere, I don't know where, and managed to get her free. Except for a part of her skirt stuck under a ceiling beam, so heavy it wouldn't budge. I was trying to tear the skirt with my teeth when I heard Mum say, "Ruth, find Father . . . Young. Tell him . . . "

I didn't understand. "Who? Tell him what?" I kept asking, and "Where's Duncan? Is he in the house?" But she never answered.

By then there were soldiers coming and I yelled for them to help. One of them took Mum's pulse and shook his head. He used a knife to cut her skirt loose, carried her out and put her inside a delivery wagon. Another soldier asked me for her name and address. I couldn't think clearly, but I must have told him because he wrote something down. I think he asked for my name, too, but I was frantic about Duncan and was already going back inside the wreckage.

The soldiers followed, yelling for me to stop, the fire was spreading, but I didn't.

I went in from the other side, the living-room side, and saw that the piano had collapsed. Someone was trapped underneath. I saw their hand.

Duncan.

It couldn't be Ruth. She'd gone off to her job at the telephone company, and Mum had thought *I* was Ruth. So it had to be Duncan.

I started to scream. A soldier picked me up and carried me out, said it wasn't safe, the fire was spreading too fast. Seconds later the piano was in flames and the other walls came crashing down.

I tried to go back. I was screaming, "My brother! He's still alive! You can lift up the piano!" but the soldier held me tight. "No one could survive that," he said.

I can't go on.

Wednesday, December 12

I didn't want to write this morning. I limped down the corridor, trying to put a bit of weight on my foot, but mostly used the cane, and tried to avoid bumping into people.

The corridor is always crowded. People looking for their families, soldiers carrying away bodies, doctors, nurses, volunteers, coming and going, coming and going.

Helen changed the dressing on my foot and said the wound is healing. The swelling has gone down. Same with my cheek. She gave me a peppermint to suck on.

I let her read my diary. All she had time for was what I wrote yesterday, but now she knows the worst, and why it's so hard for me to speak. But I can still write, and I'm determined to finish my composition.

So, Luke, here is the next part.

Charlotte's Composition, Part 3: Thursday, December 6, 1917

Our house was in flames.

A soldier was holding me, telling me that no one could survive, and suddenly everyone stopped what they were doing and started to run. "It's Wellington Barracks! The magazine's on fire! It's going to explode!" People were crying, hysterical, and soldiers were shouting, "Leave the area! Go to open spaces!" They were knocking on doors and warning everyone to get out before the next explosion.

People who could barely walk had to drag themselves outside, stumbling, or leaning on others.

An old man in his nightclothes, hobbling along on crutches, kept saying, "The Germans done this, the Germans done this," over and over until another man told him to shut up, it wasn't the Germans, it was the *Mont-Blanc* burning in the harbour — a *munitions* ship.

A little Negro girl from Africville took hold of my hand. She was clutching a doll and crying for her mother, but I didn't know what to do, just held her hand and went on.

There was a barricade at the edge of the ruined area. Dozens of people had been wanting to go in to help, or to look for someone, but now they were being turned away. When they found out the reason, there was more panic.

Streets were clogged with horse-drawn

carts, fish trucks, wagons, motor cars, motor trucks, anything that could carry away the injured and the dead, all trying to turn around and get away before the next explosion.

The Commons, and the slopes leading up to the Citadel, were crawling with people, like ants stirred out of an ant hill. Moving about in confusion, huddling by small fires, standing in groups, praying, searching, waiting, calling out names . . .

The girl with the doll spotted her mother and went running off.

I just stood there.

After a while I forced myself to move, praying I'd find Dad or Edith or Ruth. Because I didn't know then what I know now.

My bare foot was bleeding from broken glass and I was trembling all over. I sank down on the ground and reached into my pocket for my diary.

My latest entry was December 6, that very morning, but I couldn't bring myself to read it.

So I stared at the town clock and prayed. *Please God, let this not be happening . . .*

Eddie with the one arm just brought me some bread and cheese. He's nineteen. I showed him the letter Luke wrote in my diary.

I'm still thinking about the people who were trapped in the ruins. What happened to them when their rescuers were forced to leave? Duncan could have been saved. There was so much wreckage, the piano could have collapsed on top of something else, something that was protecting him. I couldn't see clearly because of the smoke and the plaster dust, but if the soldiers had put out the fire, if they'd moved the piano . . .

Thursday, December 13

My heart's about to burst, it's beating so hard, and my hands are shaking, but I have to write this down before I forget.

I woke up to the sound of my own screaming. "Duncan! Get Duncan! He's trapped inside!"

Nobody in the ward seems to be awake, so the screaming must have been part of my dream. I was in our house. The roof had caved in to the second floor and the second floor smashed down to the first, and down to the basement and everyone was buried. I saw a hand and heard a cry.

Duncan. Pinned under a beam.

I took Dad's handsaw, tried to cut through the beam, but with every cut the wood closed back in, and the house was on fire, the flames coming closer, and Duncan shrieking but I couldn't save him, the wood kept closing in. Then another voice, "Save me, get me out!" but I was surrounded by flames and I *couldn't*. Someone was pulling me and a voice was screaming, "Duncan! Get Duncan!" — my voice, and that's what woke me up.

And now I remember. It came to me, sudden and clear. *Ruth's locket.* I saw it in the dream. I'd seen it in the ruins, beside the hand, but there was so much wreckage, it didn't register. And now I *know*. I know it wasn't Duncan under the piano.

It was Ruth.

Something must have happened with her telephone-company job, or she changed her mind and went home. That's why Mum kept saying her name. She knew that Ruth was in the house.

I think the dream was a message, telling me that Duncan is still alive.

Late Thursday afternoon

I slept for a long time after writing down my dream. When I woke up again, it was time for tomato soup and a visit from a special children's committee. Two nice ladies with a list of questions.

This time I managed to speak, although my voice was barely more than a whisper. There were so many questions. Name, age, address, religion, church, school? Names of parents, brothers, sisters? Relatives in Halifax, relatives in Nova Scotia, relatives in Canada, relatives overseas?

No, no, no, no.

I told them what Mum had said at the end, and they're going to put a notice in the paper about Father Young because they didn't recognize the name. They told me that Luke might be sent home on "compassionate leave" because I'm an orphan now and he's my only adult relative. And since he's been wounded, he might be able to continue his recovery here in Canada. But I'm not to get my hopes up.

I told them about Duncan. I'm not sure they believed me, but they said there have been miracles, with people thought dead turning up alive, and they're going to put a notice in the paper that says *Urgent Contact Requested.*

After they left I took my corridor walk, this time without the cane. My bandaged foot is still sore.

Tomorrow I'm leaving the hospital. I remember how scared I was about coming here, but now I'm afraid to leave.

Thursday evening

A few minutes ago, on my way back from the bathroom, I passed Eddie and another soldier-patient talking to a tall, white-bearded man. The man was holding a walking stick with a silver knob shaped like a dragon.

Dragon Man. Duncan's drawing come to life. It wasn't a hallucination, not like some of the patients are having, and it wasn't a dream. I was awake, so it *had* to be real.

Now I'm thinking about Duncan's drawing and our book. If Dragon Man is real, then Charlotte the Fearless is real. She *can't* be afraid. She must do whatever it takes to carry on. She must find Duncan the Brave.

Later

Duncan *wasn't* at home when the explosion happened, and now I have proof.

I went for another corridor walk, but this time I went into the wards. I'd just gone into a ward on the second floor when I heard someone call my name.

It was Carl. His leg was smashed above the ankle and his head was badly cut. He was lifted off his feet by the explosion and landed on a fence.

He told me that Duncan had come to fetch him just after the *Mont-Blanc* caught fire. They were on their way to the harbour to watch the burning ship, but had no sooner got to the bottom of Carl's street when everything blew up.

That was all he could tell me, but at least I know where Duncan was that morning. It's a start.

Everyone in Carl's family was badly cut but they all survived.

I'll miss Helen when I leave the hospital. Today she brought me a sweater she'd outgrown, a flannelette nightgown, and some warm socks and mittens.

Friday, December 14

I woke up a couple of hours ago thinking, *I can tell Mum and Dad about Duncan, they'll be so happy.* Then it hit me. The hurt was so sharp I couldn't bear to face anyone, so I pulled the soldier's greatcoat over my head and pretended to be asleep. Then I went to sleep for real.

The children's committee ladies have just come by and I gave them a new notice about Duncan. I wrote it last night.

MISSING — Duncan Blackburn. 12 years, dark hair, blue eyes. Wore brown pants, long black socks and brown tweed coat. Morning of explosion was on or near Campbell at Warden. Notify Information Bureau.

I remember his clothing because it's what I wore on Hallowe'en.

Now it's time to put on my outside clothes.

Late afternoon

I'm at the Chisholms' house. It was damaged, but it's outside the area where everything was destroyed.

There are fourteen of us here. Muriel, her mum, her granny, her three brothers and baby sister, two aunts, one uncle and three little cousins, and we're living in the four rooms that aren't too badly damaged. They've put tarpaper over the missing windows and a blanket where the front door used to be.

Right now I'm sitting in a corner out of everybody's way. It's cold, and snowing heavily, so everyone's inside.

It was good to see Muriel, but it's strange living in her house. If only our house, if Mum and Dad —

I have to stop thinking "if only." It's hard *not* to think that way, when every little thing is a reminder, but I have to try.

Everything I'm wearing used to belong to someone else (except for the long woollen underwear, which is new). Fleece-lined boots, stockings, brown corduroy dress, furry hat, a black sealskin coat that's warm but too long. I don't suppose everything came from one girl, but from several. Could we have been friends? Maybe. But maybe they don't live in Halifax, or even in Nova Scotia. Mrs. Chisholm said that some of these clothes might have come from Boston or Vancouver or Montreal, because people from all over are helping out.

It felt odd wearing someone else's clothes until I remembered that Mum was always fixing up Ruth's hand-me-downs for me to wear. Or Edith's. But that was different.

My head feels different with my hair cut off. Even my skin feels different.

The only part of the old me is my diary.

This morning I left the hospital. Muriel's Uncle

Jim came for me. We went in his friend's motor car because of the storm and because I can't walk very far.

Muriel's relatives told me to call them Auntie and Uncle and Granny. "We're all family here," Uncle Jim said.

His two brothers were killed at the foundry and a sister at the textile company.

Mrs. C. doesn't know what happened to Kirsty or Billy the Pig, but she told me that the S.P.C. is taking care of animals that are homeless or injured.

Baby Ethel was saved by a miracle. She was asleep in her crib upstairs when the windows shattered. There was a window blind in the room, and it blew out in front of the glass and draped itself over the crib. The splinters of glass slid right over the top of the baby, and she woke up without a scratch.

Muriel's granny keeps saying, "An angel lay down that blind. The hands of an angel."

Why does God save some and not others? How does He decide? In the Lord's Prayer we say to Our Father, "Thy will be done on Earth as it is in Heaven." Does that mean the Explosion was God's will? Why would He do that?

It's almost time for supper. I'll do what I can to help.

Mrs. Chisholm took me to the morgue. It's in Chebucto Road School, in the basement, because there's no room at the undertaker's.

I felt numb. As if the real me was somewhere else, watching another Charlotte do what had to be done. That was the only way I could bear it. The only way I can write about it is by being straightforward with the facts and not stopping to think.

We went inside and saw row upon row of cloth-covered bodies. Each one had a number.

Mum's body was already identified because I'd given her name to the soldier, the one who was there when she died. Dad and Edith had been identified, too, by Mrs. Chisholm and by Charlie's friend.

It was different with Ruth.

Luke, when you're reading this — do you remember when the *Titanic* went down? Haggarty explained to me about identifying the bodies, and now it's the same. If a person was too badly burned or crushed to be identified, the workers in the morgue write down the place where the body was found and a description of all the "effects" that were found with it. They put the description and the effects in a cloth bag.

Then they give it the same number as the one on the body.

There were many, many bags to look through, but I finally found the one with Ruth's locket. Then I knew the remains were hers.

Now that the bodies have been identified, they can be "released" to the family, which is me, and have a proper burial. Mrs. Chisholm has arranged for the coffins. The burial will be tomorrow morning.

I have their personal possessions, and will keep them for Duncan and Luke. It breaks my heart to see how little is left. Dad's watch, Mum's plain gold wedding band, Edith's engagement ring, the clothes they were wearing. A few items found in pockets, like coins, a comb, a set of keys. Nothing in Ruth's bag but her locket.

Mrs. Chisholm thought we should make certain that Duncan wasn't there, in spite of my dream. I refused to look, so she did it for me. She started to cry on the way home and hasn't stopped since. She said it was heart-wrenching to see me suffer through such an ordeal, and without shedding a tear. She said I showed courage and strength beyond my years.

I couldn't tell her that Mum always thought I was old beyond my years. Or that my heart seizes up tight and won't let me cry.

Sunday, December 16

All the churches in Richmond were destroyed, so the funeral service couldn't be at St. Mark's. Reverend LeMoine went to the cemetery with me this morning and said a short service over the graves. Mrs. Chisholm, Muriel, Uncle Jim and Auntie Belle went, too. When we got back to the Chisholms', the grown-ups told the little ones not to bother me, but I told them I didn't mind. Their distractions make things easier.

Late afternoon

Almost the end of a very hard day. Like yesterday. I go through the motions as if I'm far away and watching someone else, feeling as if I'm walking in my sleep. Numb with a sadness too big to put into words. I can still write about other things, though, and that helps to keep my mind occupied.

So, this afternoon I went to the Food Depot with Muriel and Uncle Jim. My foot is mending well. It feels better and the bandage isn't so bulky. My "new" boots feel good because they're already broken in.

There were volunteers working at the Food Depot, even though today's Sunday. They loaded our sleds with boxes of food.

On the way back we stopped for a look at the devastated area, but we couldn't get in without a pass. I didn't want to anyway.

Most of the wreckage was covered by snow, and soldiers, sailors and volunteers were hard at work, Sunday or not. They were digging with shovels or with their bare hands, searching for bodies. There's no hope now of finding survivors.

I was surprised that there were trees still standing, and odd things — like a row of fence posts that had marked the edge of somebody's yard, but nothing left of the house except for a pile of chimney bricks. I couldn't make out where our house had been, or any of the streets.

The sugar refinery and other tall buildings along the harbour had collapsed, so we could see clear across to the far shore. We saw a wrecked ship lying there that Uncle Jim said was the *Imo*. The *Mont-Blanc* was blown to pieces.

Just as we were leaving, I did notice something I recognized. The wrought-iron gate in Miss Tebo's yard. Still standing, all by itself.

After supper

Muriel and I have finished the washing up, and I'm sitting in a corner with my diary. There's just one part left to write about that horrible day.

Charlotte's Composition, Part 4: Thursday, December 6, 1917

The second explosion never happened.

Soldiers went around telling everyone that the fire at the magazine at Wellington Barracks was out and there wasn't any danger. So after two or three hours in the cold, people began to leave.

I didn't know where to go so I stayed where I was.

After a while I got up. I felt a stab of pain in my foot — the first time I'd noticed any pain — and sank back down. The soldier who'd carried me out of my house had said I should go to a hospital, but I didn't think I was hurt badly enough, not like some, and didn't want to go.

There on the hill, for the first time, I took stock of myself. Shredded clothing plastered to my skin with sooty tar and blood. Foot swollen and bleeding. I felt something sharp in my cheek, and when I reached up, my hand came away sticky.

I kept thinking, what if Edith or Dad or Ruth turn up at the house, looking for me? What if they don't? What will I do? Where will I go? I wanted to cry but felt frozen. Not cold, but numb. Like the hands on the town clock that never moved past 9:05.

A short time later, a group of soldiers came along. One of them wrapped his greatcoat around me, said I was in shock and injured, and they were taking me to the hospital.

I was afraid. I'd never been in a hospital before and tried to push the soldier away. But he picked me up and carried me down the hill to a motor car. My first time in a motor car.

I must have fainted, because the next thing I knew, I was waking up on the floor in Camp Hill Hospital, wrapped in the soldier's greatcoat.

He must have put my diary in one of the pockets, because that's where I found it, along with a pencil. The pencil must be his. I hope he won't mind me using it.

That's the end of my composition, as best as I can remember.

Luke, when you're reading this, the soldier's coat is draped over and around me like a tent. A private space for when I'm writing. It smells of peppermints and tobacco. I pretend it's yours.

It made a good extra blanket in the hospital. Here, too. Muriel says it's heavy and scratchy, but it makes me feel protected.

Later

I've just said a prayer for Duncan. I don't know where he can be. If he's in Halifax, in a shelter or hospital, the Relief Committee would know. They would've told me by now. Wouldn't they?

The dream I had in the hospital — could I have been mistaken? What if it wasn't a message after all?

No, I'm sure I would *know* if Duncan wasn't alive. I would feel it in every bone. And yet, *before* I had that dream, I was certain it was Duncan under the piano.

Monday, December 17

Last night, when I was in the middle of finishing my composition, Muriel yanked the diary out of my hands and yelled, "You and that diary! That's all you ever do! There's food to get and chores and kids to look after, and Mum's sick with grief and we're all hurting, not just you! You're supposed to be helping, not wasting your time!"

It wasn't true and she knew it, but I was too tired to argue. "I'm doing this for Luke," I said. "So he'll know what happened."

"Luke?" she shouted. "Luke's probably dead like everybody else!"

Her words crushed me to the heart. I must have gasped or cried out, because she burst into tears, said she was sorry, she hadn't meant it, she knew Luke was safe in the hospital, anyway, and gave me back my diary.

Muriel won't talk about the Explosion, but I know she misses her dad as much as I miss mine. Sometimes she cries at night, but quietly, so she won't wake anyone up. I hug her until she calms down.

Later

After Muriel's outburst I couldn't write for a while because it's true what she said. Luke may never come home. He must have gotten Charlie's telegram by now, but what if the army doesn't give him leave? What if his bronchitis got worse? What if he's been sent back to France and has to fight another battle, even with a broken leg?

But there's no way of knowing, and nothing I can do, so I picked up my pencil and carried on.

There's a public funeral today for the unidentified dead, with services for all the different faiths. The grown-ups have gone, except for Auntie Belle. Muriel and I are helping her look after the little ones.

I couldn't face going to the funeral, but I'm praying for the dead all the same. And for Duncan and Luke, as always.

Later

This afternoon I went to the Green Lantern with Muriel. It used to be a restaurant, but now it's a clothing depot. There were two long line-ups, one with people donating things, the other with people picking things up.

Two ladies ahead of us were talking about the heavy losses, how many dead from here, how many from there. "They're saying some two hundred are gone from St. Mark's parish alone," one said. "About four hundred from St. Joseph's," said the other.

They went on to talk about Grove Presbyterian and probably the Methodist Church as well, but I stopped listening.

A little later, when they'd stopped talking, I asked if they knew of a Father Young. But they didn't.

Some people behind us were talking about the funeral this morning, and how heart-breaking it was to see the row of small coffins, each one holding the bones of several different people.

I still haven't seen what I look like. But while we were standing in line a boy walked by, took one look at my face and quickly turned away. I guess I don't need a mirror now. His look said everything.

We got two boxes of clothing for Muriel's brothers and cousins and also a box for ourselves. Muriel was hoping to get a sealskin coat like mine, but got a blue woollen one instead. So we traded.

Tuesday, December 18

Kirsty is here! She's curled up beside me in my greatcoat tent, practically in my lap! Here's what happened.

I went to Camp Hill Hospital to get my stitches out and saw Helen. She showed me a notice in the paper that said there were ten dogs who needed homes, and some of the dogs were spaniels.

She said that if I didn't mind waiting, she'd take me to the kennel to have a look as soon as her shift was over. She remembers Kirsty from the piano days, and knows that Kirsty's a Brittany spaniel, but warned me not to get my hopes up. Well it was a long wait but I didn't mind.

On the way to the kennel I *tried* not to get my hopes up, but sure enough, there she was!

The minute she saw me her ears cocked up and she made her happy *arroo* sounds, her whole body quivering with joy. I sank to my knees and hugged her, my face pressed against her side, sobbing with relief, until her fur was wet with tears. It's the first time I've been able to cry, even the slightest bit.

Kirsty limps from the cuts on her paws, and her fur has streaks of oily soot, but she looks perfect to me.

Now that I have something good to say, I'm going to write a letter to Luke. I couldn't manage before, but now I think I can.

Wednesday, December 19

Heavy snowfall, terrible wind. Muriel and I went to the Food Depot with Uncle Jim, and Kirsty came, too.

We got bread and milk and canned goods and

so on, and pulled everything back on our sleds. Muriel's brothers took one look at the maple leaf cookies and started whining, "Not again, we're sick of maple cookies," until Mrs. C. had had enough. Then it was shouting, tears, more shouting, more tears until I wanted to scream. I didn't, though, just escaped inside my greatcoat tent with my diary and Kirsty.

Yesterday the boys were squabbling over the one *green* sweater that Mrs. Chisholm brought back from the relief depot, the depot with the piles of goods sent from Massachusetts. She and the aunts went early and came back with fur coats for Granny and themselves, sweaters for everyone (including me) and a baby layette for Ethel. Except for the boys, everyone was satisfied.

Later

Some people from the committee in charge of shelter came this afternoon and said that the Chisholms' house is too crowded, too cold, and too unsafe. Everyone has to stay somewhere else until the house is repaired.

When they told me I'd be moving to a Mrs. Kessler's house, I said that I couldn't leave the Chisholms' because how would Duncan find me?

They said it's all been arranged and I don't need to worry because they'll know where I am.

The Kesslers want to give some children a home over Christmas. I'm allowed to take Kirsty tomorrow, but it's up to the Kesslers to decide whether or not she can stay. They *have* to let her!

Muriel and the others are going to Saint John to stay with different relatives. They could have gone after the Explosion but wanted to stay together. Now the family will be split up because the New Brunswick relatives don't have enough room for everybody.

It surprised me to hear mention of Christmas. Every day I write the date in my diary, but I hadn't made the connection. I don't want a Christmas anyway.

Thursday, December 20

I'm writing this in the Kesslers' house. It's a big warm house on Spring Garden Road, near the Public Gardens.

The walls are standing and the roof is on. The windows are out, like everywhere else, with boards and tarpaper and blankets to keep out the cold.

The Kesslers have a cat called Snowball and a

parrot called Crackers. They're letting Kirsty stay. Snowball doesn't look pleased. Crackers doesn't seem to care.

There are three boys and three girls here. Matthew, Kevin, Lewis, Sarah, Sophie and me. I'm the oldest and Sophie is the youngest. She's four.

There are lots of toys and books that people have donated. More toys than we've ever seen except in the stores. There's even a dollhouse that Mrs. Kessler had when she was a little girl. It's got fancy furnishings and real glass windows that didn't break in the explosion.

A neighbour came over and set up an electric train, with tracks and tunnels and a station, and Mrs. Kessler's niece donated three of her porcelain dolls.

Kirsty's been following me everywhere. Poor dog. She's been with so many strangers and in so many different places, she can't bear to let me out of her sight. When I'm in the bathroom she sits outside the door and whimpers until I come out.

For dessert tonight we had *blanc mange* with corn syrup. I was all set to have some until I remembered it was the way Mum used to make it. Then I was too sad to eat.

Almost forgot. Yesterday I said goodbye to my

"greatcoat tent." I gave it to the committee to return to the soldier. His name was inside the coat, on a label. I put a thank-you note in the pocket and said I was sorry I'd kept it for so long.

Friday, December 21

Shredded Wheat Biscuits for breakfast. The first time I've had them.

Sarah and I helped Mrs. Kessler do the breakfast dishes.

After that I walked to the Bellevue Building on Spring Garden Road to see Haggarty. The Stars and Stripes are flying outside the building because some people from Boston turned it into a hospital, and American doctors and nurses are working there. Now it's called the American Bellevue Hospital.

Kirsty came but had to wait outside.

I found Haggarty. He knew of my loss and hugged me tight. No need for words. But didn't he brighten when I told him about Kirsty. Maybe we can live with the Haggartys until Luke comes home. Duncan, too. Mrs. Haggarty wasn't injured in the Explosion, being at home on the other side of Fort Needham, but Haggarty lost an eye.

"At least it wasn't the left one," he said. "Otherwise I'd have to learn to wink all over again."

134

He can't decide whether to wear a black patch "for the buccaneer look," or have a glass eye put in. And if he goes for a glass eye, what colour? What about a design, like the Stars and Stripes "in honour of the good Bostonians"?

It felt good to see him and listen to his banter.

I even surprised myself by teasing him. "Please tell me your name," I said (not letting on that I knew).

"Long John Silver," he says.

"No, your *real* name."

"Call me anything you like, but don't call me late for dinner."

We had a good laugh, and then I said, "Can I call you Ethelbert?"

Oh, he was mortified. "You cheeky monkey!" he says.

And Kirsty, left outside for twenty minutes! *Everyone* in the hospital must have heard the howls, because Haggarty and I sure did.

For a short time I forgot my sadness. But when I got back, and Mrs. Kessler made me some cocoa . . . I heard Dad's voice and the sadness came rushing back.

Later

Duncan's alive and safe and well! I knew it, just like in my dream, and tomorrow he'll be in Halifax. My hand's shaking, I can hardly write for relief and excitement, but here's what happened.

Earlier today a nurse in Truro telephoned the Information Bureau and told them that Duncan Blackburn was a patient there, and was asking about his sister, and did they know anything, and they said they did. So a lady came over — she's only just left — and told me that Duncan will be here tomorrow, right here at the Kesslers'!

Saturday, December 22

11:00 p.m.

Oh, where to start?

The house is quiet, everyone's asleep, but I'm too stirred up to go to bed because Duncan is here!

The minute I saw him I started to cry, and I've hardly stopped since. Before the Kesslers went upstairs, Mrs. Kessler gave me two dry handkerchiefs and said I could stay up as long as I liked.

Here's what happened.

Duncan showed up this morning and oh, the

hugs and tears, his surprise at seeing Kirsty, her delight in greeting him with slobbery wet kisses — well we were beside ourselves with emotion.

Mrs. Kessler and Mrs. O'Neill, the lady who brought him, did a fair bit of of weeping, too.

And when he finally catches his breath, the first thing Duncan says? "Charlotte! I've been in Truro!" As if he's been off on an excursion.

Well I cried and laughed and cried some more because at first I'm thinking, Doesn't he know what happened?

Well he knows, all right. I could tell by the fierce way he hugged me, the bewildered look in his eyes and the tremor in his voice when he said, "We're the only ones left, aren't we? You and me and Luke."

It's only because he was amazed at finding himself in Truro in the first place, that his earlier words came out sounding the way they did.

He said I could write his story in my diary, if I wanted to record it for Luke, but he wouldn't write it himself. He said he'd tell me what happened to him and that would be the end of it. He would never speak of it again.

Luke, when you're reading this, it was hard enough writing my own story, but you'll want to know about Duncan. And so I agreed.

Duncan's Story:
December 6–21, 1917

The morning of December 6, Duncan was looking out his bedroom window and saw the *Imo* and *Mont-Blanc* heading straight for each other in the Narrows. When the *Mont-Blanc* caught fire, he went to get Carl so the two of them could go to the harbour for a closer look.

He thinks he and Carl had just turned onto Campbell Street when the explosion happened. He remembers seeing a white flash. But the next thing he knew, it was three days later and he was in a hospital bed in Truro.

He doesn't remember how he got there. A nurse told him he'd been found in a daze, stumbling down the railway tracks leading out of Richmond. Someone had carried him to the No. 10 train, and the train had taken him to Truro along with hundreds of other injured people. (No. 10 was coming in from Saint John and had already passed Truro when the explosion happened, but had managed to make its way to a spot between Africville and Richmond.)

Duncan was unconscious by the time he got to Truro, probably because of a blow on his head. A cut on his forehead took seven stitches to close, but he had no other serious cuts and no broken bones.

When the nurse first saw him, his skin was so black she thought he was from Africville. He couldn't tell the nurses or doctors anything, being unconscious, but even after he woke up he couldn't. Name, address, age? He didn't know. Parents, brothers, sisters? He didn't know.

He drew a lot of pictures. A dragon with a human head and flames coming out of its mouth. A girl and a boy and a dog flying above the flames. He told everyone that Dragon Man was coming and he had to be ready. The doctors and nurses said he was delirious.

Mrs. O'Neill was a volunteer at the hospital. When she was here, she told us that the hospital had sent a description of Duncan to Halifax the day after the explosion but had never heard back. It may well have gone astray or been lost. Most of Duncan's clothes had been blown off by the blast, and the rest had been in tatters, so the only description was of his approximate age and size and the colour of his eyes and hair.

It was almost two weeks before he could remember anything. Mrs. O'Neill was changing the dressing on his forehead when he told her his name was Duncan, and he had a twin sister called Charlotte. It was the first time his words had made any sense, but it was another day before he could give them all the information they needed.

So a nurse telephoned the Information Bureau and here he is.

I can hardly keep my eyes open . . .

Sunday, December 23

Duncan and I went to St. Paul's this morning, with Mrs. Kessler. Reverend LeMoine gave a special service for the parishioners of St. Mark's, because of our church being destroyed.

St. Paul's is where the Kesslers go to church. The windows were broken in the blast, and debris was embedded in the walls. The church hall has been turned into a hospital and dressing station. There's a big Red Cross banner outside.

Rev. LeMoine was happy to see Duncan. He asked what news we had of Luke, but I didn't have anything to tell him.

There's still no word about Father Young. Reverend LeMoine has never heard of him. I'm starting to think I was delirious and imagined Mum's words.

The little ones here have taken a great liking to Duncan. He draws pictures of them flying in the treetops or fishing in the clouds. He's given them names like Matthew the Mighty and Sophie the Courageous, and told them they can all be in our new book. He tells everyone that my name is Charlotte the Fearless. And together we're the Intrepidous Twins.

Later

Duncan has just told me something he'd forgotten. The day of the explosion, when he was on his way to get Carl, he saw Ruth. She'd gone to the telephone company to start her job, but somehow they'd found out she wasn't sixteen and sent her home.

Duncan told her that we'd known about her plans all along. He swore we'd kept it a secret, but she didn't believe him, and put all the blame on me. She said she'd kill me when she got home.

Duncan asked if she wanted to go to the harbour with him and Carl, and watch the burning ship, but she didn't. She went home instead.

I'm sad to think that Ruth's last thoughts of me were full of anger and blame.

Monday, December 24

8:30 p.m.

This morning Sophie came to me in tears and said, "Tomorrow's Christmas and I'm not

Luke is coming home! I'm giddy with excitement, and no wonder, because it's the best Christmas present Duncan and I could have imagined, and to get the news on Christmas Eve, only ten minutes ago — well, my heart is overflowing!

I'd scarcely even started today's entry when a man came to the door with an army telegram saying that Luke is on his way home. We don't know when he left England, but at least it's official. *Oh tidings of comfort and joy!*

Later

Now it's 9:15 p.m. I've had some cocoa with Duncan, Matthew and Sarah, and managed to calm down — not much, but enough to finish my entry for today.

So back to this morning, and Sophie in tears. Poor little thing. "Tomorrow's Christmas, and I'm not at home," she said. "Santa won't know where I am."

She was so sweet and earnest, I burst into tears myself, on the inside. But on the outside, I put on a brave face and told her that Santa knows where she is because Santa knows everything.

Then came the questions. Are you sure? Does he know you're here? Does he know Duncan's here? Does he know Matthew's here?

Yes, yes, yes — On it went for everyone in the house, including Mrs. Kessler, Mr. Kessler, Snowball, Crackers and Kirsty.

Then she asked if the chimney was still on the roof.

I told her there were two chimneys, so Santa could take his pick, but she had to see for herself.

She was relieved when she looked up and saw the chimneys, straight and tall, not one brick out of place, but I began to worry. Because what if I'd spoken too soon and Santa didn't come?

Mrs. Kessler reassured me. "Santa will indeed be paying us a visit," she said, and gave me such a warm motherly hug I wanted to cry. But I didn't, because the little ones see me as strong and fearless.

In the afternoon Mr. Kessler brought home an enormous tree. He had to stand on a chair to put the angel on top, and almost fell over.

The angel made me think of Muriel's baby sister, so I told everyone the story. Mrs. Kessler looked at us and said, "There was an angel guarding each and every one of you that day."

Then she put us to work. Holly and ivy here, boughs of cedar there, candles on the mantle, candles on the tree, ornaments hanging from every branch, now let's set up the Nativity Scene, how about some carols, oh, look at Snowball playing with the tinsel, and so on. We were kept so busy there was almost no time for sadness.

After supper we sat by the fire and sang some more carols and listened to Mr. Kessler recite "A Visit from Saint Nicholas." Then he gave us each a stocking to hang by the fireplace. Sophie put out the milk and cookies for Santa and the little ones went to bed.

Now it's time for me to do the same, but how will I ever get to sleep?

Very late

Oh, the Christmas memories. And Luke coming home. I woke up with my head spinning and couldn't get back to sleep, so I got out of bed and tiptoed downstairs. Now I'm writing at the kitchen table. I'm tempted to peek inside the living room to see if Santa has come, but I won't.

Luke, when you're reading this, remember how the whole family used to read *A Christmas Carol* and take on different roles? And how Ruth always had to be Scrooge? She really was good! I wish I'd told her.

And remember how Dad would recite the Christmas story every Christmas Eve? Oh, his voice. The part with the shepherds abiding in the fields, "And Lo, the angel of the Lord came upon them and the glory of the Lord shone round about them . . . " It still makes me shiver with wonder.

Remember the Christmas parties? Our little house bulging with friends and neighbours and everyone with an instrument and a voice, dancing, singing — and the time Duncan's loose tooth comes out and he's showing it off and drops it in the punch bowl!

And the time . . .

Oh, now I'm too sleepy to go on. I hope my cot doesn't creak when I go back to bed because I don't want Sophie and Sarah to wake up, thinking I'm Santa.

Tomorrow will be hard. I know that Mum and

Dad and Ruth and Edith are in heaven. But how I wish they were here.

Tuesday, December 25

7:00 Christmas night. I'm already half asleep.

Sophie woke everyone this morning. "Santa came! Just like Charlotte said! Come and see!"

There was a stack of beautifully wrapped presents under the tree. More than I've ever seen. The stockings were bulging with nuts and candies and oranges.

Mr. Kessler played Santa and handed out the presents. After we opened them we had breakfast. Then we went to church.

We had a turkey dinner, but I wasn't hungry. I felt bad that I hadn't given Mr. and Mrs. Kessler a present. They've been so kind.

Everyone did their best to be merry, for the little ones, but it was a sad Christmas.

I'm glad it's over.

Wednesday, December 26

Went to Citadel Hill with Duncan, Matthew and Sarah. Mr. Kessler let us take his toboggan.

We had a few good runs, until the toboggan sped out of control and plowed into a snowbank.

Lucky it was only a snowbank, because on the way down we almost hit three ladies, a couple of soldiers, two boys on a sled and several dogs, including Kirsty. If Duncan hadn't steered us into the snowbank we might've shot right over to the Commons and crashed into one of the new apartments they're building for the people who lost their homes.

As we were getting up and shaking off the snow, I heard a familiar laugh. I turned around and sure enough, it was Eva!

Well we laughed and hugged and cried, and laughed some more, and walked arm in arm about the Commons, talking talking talking.

At first we skirted around the Explosion, wanting to know, but not wanting to know, about each other's families. But I could feel the question hanging between us, and finally told her about my family. Oh, the tears.

Eva's family was lucky. Her dad and Werner were downstairs in the store, nailing a sheet of beaverboard over the window that had been broken by hooligans the night before. It turned out that the broken window was a good thing, because the force of the explosion knocked Werner, Mr. Heine and the board backwards, with no cut faces because they'd already removed the glass.

Eva and her mum had seen the burning ship from an upstairs window, and were running downstairs to tell the others when the explosion happened. They were thrown down the staircase and found themselves on the floor with canned goods and so on all around them. Eva landed on a broken bottle of syrup and got a bad gash on her leg, and her mum got a fractured wrist. They all got out before the building caught on fire.

Three days after the explosion, Eva's dad was arrested for being a German, but they let him go.

Thank heavens I saw her today. They've been living with her mum's cousin in the South End, but tomorrow they're going to Montreal to stay with her dad's sister. They're planning to come back to Halifax in the summer.

We promised we'd write to each other. "Long letters," Eva said, "with a new limerick every week." That made us cry some more, remembering.

Late afternoon

Just before supper, Eva and her mum came calling. They gave me their address in Montreal, and I gave them Mrs. Kessler's.

I may not be here by the time Eva writes, but

Mrs. K. said she'd be sure to get the letter to me. *Where will I be?* Such a big question. I'm not worried though, because what can I do? Everything about my life is in someone else's hands. Besides, I don't really care where I am, as long as I'm with Duncan. And Kirsty.

Thursday, December 27

Today Mr. Kessler handed out spades and shovels and we played Treasure Hunt. There wasn't any gold to find, only coal, but it was fun.

"Must be a ton of coal out there," Mr. K. told us. Because last fall, whenever the neighbours' dogs or cats came around to bully Snowball, he'd throw chunks of coal to scare them off. Along the fence, back of the shed, over by the clothesline pole — he had a story for every cat or dog he hit (but mostly missed).

We made snow angels before the yard got too dug up, and threw snowballs, and discovered over two dozen chunks of coal.

After that we came inside and had fish chowder for supper.

Later

I love reading stories to Sophie and Lewis before bedtime. The others listen, too, and I pretend I'm their big sister. But tonight I made a mistake.

I was reciting "A Visit from Saint Nicholas." I almost know the whole poem by heart: *"'Twas the night before Christmas, when all through the house, not a creature was stirring, not even a mouse. The stockings were hung by the chimney with care . . . "*

Sometimes I say the lines wrong on purpose to make the little ones laugh. But tonight I said, "'Twas the *fright* before Christmas." Everyone went quiet, and Sophie whispered, "That was the Explosion."

No one talks about it, but it's with us all the time.

Friday, December 28

7:00 p.m.

I'm in the living room writing, Duncan's drawing, Mr. Kessler's reading the newspaper and Snowball is purring in his lap. Mrs. K. is knitting. Click, click . . . a sound I haven't heard in a long time.

Kirsty's sleeping with her head on my feet. I'm starting to feel pins and needles, but I don't want to disturb her. She's such a good dog.

If a stranger looked into the room, he might think we were a family.

This afternoon Duncan and I went to the Bellevue Hospital to see Haggarty. He's decided to go for the buccaneer look, and asked if we knew where he might get a parrot.

Duncan said, "Yes, but you're not getting Crackers!"

It was good to see him laugh.

Sometimes I catch him staring at nothing, and his eyes are so full of sadness I wonder if he's sorry he got back his memory. Because what better way to escape the horror than by not being able to remember? He never talks about the days he spent in that place of not knowing.

I wonder what it's like to be unconscious. Is it like being asleep but without the dreams? Is it like being dead? Maybe he was at the Gates of Heaven, and saw Mum and Dad, and he wanted to join them, but he couldn't get in because it wasn't his time.

After we got back from the Bellevue I helped Mrs. K. polish her silver. Duncan and Matthew took turns running the electric train and making

Dear Charlotte,
Thanks for letting me write in your diary.
I don't mind not getting one from Luke.
You were right. I would rather draw.
Happy Birthday!!!
Your OLDER twin,
Duncan

P.S. I'm letting the others write
something because I don't need
a whole page. I hope you don't mind.
P.P.S. Do you like Kirsty's pawprint?

God bless you, my precious girl,
Love,
Mum

Chin up, Charlotte!
All my love,
Dad

Happy birthday, little sister,
Your big bad sister,
Ruth

Dear Charlotte,
May all your dreams come true,
Your loving sister,
Edith

Saturday, December 29

Last night when I turned the page . . . I couldn't speak, not even to Duncan. It hurt so much I wanted to tear the page out.

I'm glad I didn't. Their words are a comfort now. Mum and Dad, Edith and Ruth. My guardian angels.

Sunday, December 30

Stormy, and the wind brutal cold, but what we discovered made up for the weather. Here's what happened.

Duncan and I bundled up in our warmest clothes and went into the devastated area. It's still crowded with people clearing up the ruins, and we had to get a permit before they'd let us pass.

All that's left of our house is the foundation. The rest is a heap of rubble and ashes. "She's not posh but she's paid for," Dad used to say. He was right proud of our house.

One of the volunteers digging through our basement looked at our permit and said we shouldn't have come, it was too gruesome for children.

I told him that we wanted to be there in case something was found, that there was no one else and that we were almost fourteen. (A lie, as Duncan later pointed out, but I feel much older than twelve.) I also told the man that we wanted to say goodbye to the house before every last trace was gone.

He softened up then and said we could stay for a while. Even though we really didn't have to be there in person, because anything that was found, no matter how small, we could claim later on.

So Duncan and I stood without speaking and watched the men dig through our basement.

They were everywhere, volunteers and soldiers, digging in all the ruined houses, looking for bodies and personal effects. There have been some astonishing finds. Like the unbroken pieces of a little girl's tea set, and a fragile china cup with the words *Remember Me* printed on the side. A child was found in a cellar, alive and unhurt, snuggling close to a puppy, a full day after the explosion. And a baby, with scarcely a scratch, was found under a stove. It seems she was protected by the ashpan.

In the ruins of our house, the men found some letters. They were wrapped in oilcloth and bound tightly with string, and must have been well hidden, for Duncan and I had never seen them. And how did they escape the fire?

The man who handed them to me shook his

head. "It's right holy amazing what survives," he said. "Think of it as a gift."

Well the minute we got back to the Kesslers', we started looking through the letters. There were a dozen, postmarked from 1897 to 1908, each addressed in Mum's handwriting to a Mr. and Mrs. A. D. Wakefield on Young Avenue, Halifax. All were marked *Return to Sender* and mailed back, unopened.

Wakefield was Mum's maiden name — we knew that much, at least. And the first letter was mailed in December, 1897.

Duncan said what I was thinking. "Isn't that when Luke was born?"

It was, all right. We're not likely to forget, since December 2, eighteen years later, was the very day he joined up for the war. We figured that Mum had written to some relatives to tell them about her baby.

Well, as we were checking the other postmarks, something began to dawn on me. "Duncan," I said, "what if there never was a Father Young. What if Mum was trying to tell me that her *father* lived on Young Avenue, and that I should find him, in case Dad . . . ?"

"No," Duncan said after a moment. "Mum's parents died before she got married. That's what she told us."

"But what if it wasn't true? What if she meant they were 'dead' to her?"

He said it was possible, but even so, he wouldn't go to the Wakefields. Why would they want to meet us, after returning all Mum's letters? He finished off by saying, "They can't be very nice."

"That's not the point," I told him. "It was Mum's last wish. We have to go."

So first thing tomorrow, before we change our minds, we're going to the house on Young Avenue.

Then came the big question. Should we read the letters or not?

I'm curious, but afraid of what I might discover. Duncan feels the same. If Mum's writing about Dad and our sisters, it might make us miss them even more. And what if her letters show she wasn't happy? That would make us even sadder.

Haggarty once said that what happened to Mum in the past was *her* story. I don't think I'm ready for it yet. Like Dad used to say, "Let sleeping dogs lie." That's what we're going to do.

Monday, December 31

Duncan was in a terrible state last night. What if Mr. Wakefield isn't Mum's father? What if he is, and doesn't like us?

I thought back to the Explosion and said, "What's the worst that can happen now?"

That didn't help either, so this morning I got up early and asked Mrs. Kessler for advice.

She said we should go to the Wakefields', for our mother's sake as well as for our own. Because if we didn't go, if we didn't find out for sure, we'd always be wondering. And we'd be like the other Explosion children who've lost their relatives. We'd end up being adopted by strangers or placed in an orphanage. And if we were adopted, there was no guarantee we'd be able to stay together.

She said this in a kind way, but her words came as a shock. I never thought that Duncan and I might be separated, not once we'd found each other.

She explained that the Relief Committee *wanted* to keep brothers and sisters together, and keep them in Halifax, but it wasn't always possible. She said that when the war was over, Duncan and I would be able to live with Luke, since he's an adult, but if something were to happen to him . . .

Well she offered to visit the Wakefields for us and explain our situation. If all went well, she'd accompany Duncan and me at a later time. That way, we wouldn't have to meet them on our own.

She says there's a good chance the Wakefields are our grandparents, and she's sorry that we never knew, especially since they're right in Halifax.

"Mum told us they'd passed away a long time ago," I told her. "She never talked about them and neither did Dad. I don't know why."

"I expect they had their reasons," she said. "Quarrels, differences of opinion — it happens sometimes with families. You and Duncan might be the ones to patch things up."

That was the end of our conversation. I've written it down, almost word for word, and as soon as Duncan gets up I'll let him read it for himself.

Later

Went coasting on Citadel Hill and saw Ruth's friend Hilda. She said she'd never forgive herself, that if she hadn't told her teacher on Ruth, the telephone company wouldn't have found out Ruth's age and sent her home. She'd still be alive. "Wouldn't she, Charlotte?"

I told her I didn't know. How could anyone know?

Too cold to stay outside for long, so we came home and played cards. Then the girls rearranged the furniture in the dollhouse and the boys ran the electric train. Sometimes they let the dollhouse people ride around on the train. Lewis and Kevin wanted to put the dollhouse lady on the tracks so she could be rescued in the nick of time, or run over by the train, but Duncan wouldn't let them.

After supper we made up stories to go with Duncan's pictures, and Mr. Kessler showed us some magic tricks. He can pull a quarter out of our ears.

We tried to keep busy all day, to take our minds off this Thursday. That's when everyone's leaving except for Sophie and Lewis. They're staying with the Kesslers until the end of the war, and then relatives in England will come for them. Sarah's going to an uncle's farm in New Brunswick, and Matthew and Kevin are staying at a temporary Home for Children until the Protestant Orphanage is rebuilt. Duncan and I might go there, too. But that depends on the Wakefields.

1918

Tuesday, January 1, 1918

In a few minutes we're going to Young Avenue. I didn't think I was nervous, but early this morning, when I thought I was alone in the bedroom, I caught myself praying out loud. "Please let it be all right, please let them want to take care of us . . . "

And then I heard a little voice. "Don't be scared. You're Charlotte the Fearless. You can do anything."

Sophie. She'd slipped in without my noticing and said just the right thing.

Last night Mrs. Kessler told us about the Wakefields. She went with a lady from the children's committee and said they were lucky to find the Wakefields at home. Mr. Wakefield volunteers at the YMCA and visits wounded soldiers in the hospitals. He's also on a committee that welcomes returning soldiers. Mrs. Wakefield volunteers in Victoria General Hospital and helped set up the Home for Children where Matthew and Kevin are going.

Without stopping to think, I blurted out what Muriel once told me: that people in the South End of Halifax are so snobby they won't even speak to a person who lives north of Quinpool Road. Then I had to bite my tongue because the Kesslers themselves are in the South End.

Mrs. Kessler laughed, not the least bit offended. "The Wakefields are kind-hearted people," she said, "and my colleague thought the same."

"But you're grown-ups," said Duncan. "What if they don't like children? What if they don't like us?"

Mrs. Kessler said the nicest thing. "Charlotte the Fearless, Duncan the Brave, how could they help but love you?"

I fell asleep thinking about her words.

This morning we went to the New Year's Day service at St. Paul's. Then we had a special New Year's dinner. That's all I can write because it's time to go.

Later

I'm writing in the living room, after everyone has gone to bed. Except for the Kesslers and Duncan.

It's been an eventful day. I'm desperate tired, I want to go to sleep, but I can't leave this till tomorrow because I'm sure tomorrow will be eventful, too.

This afternoon Mrs. K. took us to the house on Young Avenue. A maid answered the door and showed us into the library.

Mrs. K. made herself at home, but we felt out of place and didn't dare sit down. Instead, we stood by the fireplace and counted the loud tick-tocks of the great-grandfather clock.

After a while we heard footsteps and voices in the hallway. I knew what I wanted to say and I cleared my throat, praying that my voice would be strong, and that I'd do Mum and Dad proud.

Instead, I gasped and Duncan cried out in alarm. Because who should walk in but Dragon Man.

Our reaction was a shock to everyone. Duncan wanted to leave, I wanted to stay, Mrs. K. and the Wakefields were speechless with confusion.

I finally managed to tell them about the man I'd seen in the hospital, and how he'd reminded me of Duncan's drawings. And Duncan explained that when he was little, he'd seen Mr. Wakefield in the Public Gardens. A big man with a white beard who'd made Mum cry. That's how he got the idea of Dragon Man — but years later, when he was older.

Mr. Wakefield said he'd like to see Duncan's drawings. He told us that he and Mrs. Wakefield had some explaining of their own to do, but there'd be time enough for that after we got settled. Because it's true, they're our grandparents, and they want us to live with them. Mr. Wakefield assured us that we'd be quite safe, as he'd stopped breathing fire some time ago.

I knew that Mrs. K. had told the Wakefields about the letters, and I surprised myself by saying, "Why did you return Mum's letters? Didn't you want to read them?"

They exchanged glances, as if waiting for the other to begin. Then Mr. Wakefield explained that they had parted ways with our mother years ago. He looked uncomfortable, saying that both sides had spoken hurtful and angry words and, as time went by, it became more and more difficult to make amends. They were afraid that reading the letters would only reopen old wounds.

They had seen Mum and Dad listed among the dead, but the only Blackburn names they knew were those of our parents. They never knew about us children.

I hated them at that moment, and had to force myself not to shout, *You never wanted to know! You never bothered to find out!* Instead, I calmed myself and told them what Mum had said at the end.

Mr. Wakefield's eyes brimmed over. He looked at Duncan and me and said, "If you can forgive us, I swear to God we'll do right by your mother now."

After that, the maid served tea and fruitcake. Then we came back with Mrs. Kessler.

I'm still wondering about the letters. Give them to the Wakefields, now that it seems they've had a change of heart? Keep them myself? One day, when I'm older, I'm sure I'll want to read them.

Or I can give them to Luke. I hadn't thought of this before, but now he's the head of the family. I hope he gets here soon.

Tomorrow we're leaving the Kesslers'. One last night in this big and comfy house.

Wednesday, January 2

2:00 p.m., bright and sunny. The mercury says it's the coldest day we've had all winter, but it doesn't feel that cold. For once there's hardly any wind.

Went to St. Paul's this morning for a special memorial service to honour the dead. A huge gathering of people, silent and solemn, everyone suffering a loss. I cried during the service and all the way home, but once I got back I had to stop. There was too much to do.

First, lunch. Then helping with the dishes. Then packing my things, which didn't take long. After that I brushed Kirsty. She has to look presentable because at the last minute, I told the Wakefields we had a dog, and couldn't leave her behind. It was right bold. I should have asked permission. I hope they won't be angry.

Yesterday when we got home Duncan drew a new picture of Dragon Man. He still has the white hair and beard, and the silver dragon on his cane. But now his shoulders are stooped, his body looks frail and he's leaning heavily on the cane. Instead of breathing flames, he's smoking a pipe.

Lewis looked at the drawing and frowned. "How come Dragon Man looks different?"

"Because he's changed," says Duncan.

"He isn't scary anymore?"

"No, so we don't have to worry."

Lewis chewed on his thumb, thinking. Then he says, "I know why he's changed. He's afraid of the *intredible* twins!"

Poor Lewis, he never could say "intrepidous," but we don't mind. Especially since it's a made-up word anyway.

Here comes Mrs. Kessler. Please, not yet —

My throat's seizing up. It's time to say good-bye.

Thursday, January 3

9:00 p.m.

A ferocious blizzard is howling at the window and here I am, safe and warm, inside my mother's castle. It's like a dream . . . except that she isn't here.

I miss her and Dad so much.

Friday, January 4

I woke up in the "castle" so it wasn't a dream. I slept in Mum's room, the room she had when she was my age. I slept in her bed.

First time I've slept in a room by myself, and I was awake half the night from the strangeness. No sounds of breathing but my own.

Duncan's in the room next door. I heard him cry out in the night. He must have been having another nightmare.

Kirsty has to sleep in the mud room off the kitchen. Ellie the maid found her an old blanket to curl up on, and Mary, the cook, gave her some water and a meaty bone, but Kirsty gave me a woeful look all the same. She started to howl when we shut the door, and kept it up for some time. Poor dog.

The house isn't really a castle, although it feels that way. It's grand and beautiful, with so many rooms a person could be here a week and never see another soul. Will I ever get used to it?

Mrs. Kessler brought us here on Wednesday and oh, the tears when we said goodbye.

After she left, our grandparents took us upstairs to our bedrooms and gave us a tour of the house.

They told us we're free to wander at will, but they don't want us getting lost.

Duncan and I were too overwhelmed to speak.

Maid. Library. Grandparents. I never imagined writing those words, not in any way connected to me, or where I live.

And what words do I use to describe this place? Everything shines and sparkles. There's crystal and brass and wide curving stairs with marble railings, soft carpets in rich colours and intricate designs, burgundy velvet drapes with braided gold tassels, oil paintings in gilded frames, high, high ceilings and in the living room there's a piano — and a *Victrola!* With the little dog, just like in the ads, listening to "his master's voice."

Here in Mum's old room there's an area like a tower with windows overlooking the garden and Point Pleasant Park. Before the explosion, the tower windows were stained glass but now the glass is plain. All the broken windows in the house have been replaced.

I'm writing at the desk that sits in the tower. It's called a rolltop desk because the front rolls up into the top and disappears. It has spaces for putting things in, called pigeonholes. There's also a secret hiding place. I looked inside, hoping to find something that Mum might have hidden, but it was empty.

Ellie has just rapped on the door and told me it's time for breakfast. Mary has cooked something special.

Still Friday

7:10 p.m.

Duncan and I are sitting at the desk in the tower. We've been talking quietly and now he's drawing. The clock in this room has chimed the hour, and in five minutes it will chime the quarter-hour. I must have slept more than I thought last night, because I didn't notice the chiming. Tonight I may not be able to sleep for counting out the strokes every hour. Midnight will last forever.

We can also hear the bongs of the great-grandfather clock in the library, and the chimes of another clock in the living room. Every clock strikes the hour a few seconds apart.

Today was long and mostly silent, except for the clocks and my piano playing, and a bit of conversation at breakfast.

"What should we call you?" I asked.

Our grandparents looked surprised, as if they hadn't thought about that. Now that we're actually *here,* they probably feel as awkward as we do.

Our grandmother finally said we could call them whatever we liked.

"But not late for dinner?"

Haggarty's joke, and everyone laughed. Then it went quiet again.

The rest of the day was the same. Gran and Grandpa (that's what we decided), asked us a lot of questions. How are you feeling? Do you need anything? Is there anything special you'd like to eat? Would you like to meet some children in the area?

They never ask about the Explosion, and I'm glad about that. But why don't they ask about Mum?

Duncan says he feels her presence. I do, too. This afternoon, at the piano, I felt that she was looking over my shoulder. She's everywhere. But there's not so much as a photograph.

I finally saw my face in a mirror. There's a crescent-shaped scar on my cheek. It's purplish-blue, because of the oily rain. No matter how much I wash, the blue doesn't go away. Same with the scar on Duncan's forehead.

Almost forgot. The special breakfast this morning was griddle cakes with maple syrup, and some of Mary's scones. She's a good cook.

Saturday, January 5

8:00 p.m., the end of a long day

Took Kirsty for a walk after lunch and did some thinking. By the time I got back I'd made a decision.

I didn't stop to take off my coat, just came right out and asked the grandparents why Mum had never told us about them and why they'd parted ways in the first place.

Before they had a chance to answer, I handed them my diary. "Please read it," I said. "So you'll know who we've lost." After that I went straight back outside. Kirsty couldn't believe her good fortune. Two walks, one right after another! She nearly wagged her tail off with excitement.

We walked along Young Avenue to where it turns into South Park Street, and all the way to Spring Garden Road. From there it was only a few blocks to the American Bellevue Hospital.

Went up to see Haggarty, only to find out that he was sent home yesterday.

On the way back I realized something. Duncan and I think about Mum and Dad and our sisters all the time, but we hardly ever talk about them because it's too painful. It might be the same with our grandparents. They don't mention Mum for the same reason they didn't open the letters — because it hurts too much. Because whatever happened between them can *never* be put right, not now, and they're reminded of that whenever they look at Duncan and me. What I said to them, and the way I'd spoken, had likely made things worse. That's what I thought.

When I got back, everyone was in the library having tea. I was about to apologize, not only for my outburst but also for being late, when Gran began to talk. Grandpa, too. Before long we had the whole story.

Gran was weeping. She told us they'd wanted the best for their Lily, and when she wanted to marry a man "with no worthy prospects," they thought she was making a terrible mistake.

They objected so strongly to John Blackburn as a suitable husband, Grandpa threatened to disown her if she went through with the marriage. "We'll have no more to do with you," he'd said.

Mum's response? "Then I am no longer your daughter."

And that was that.

Grandpa had met Mum by accident in the Public Gardens, that day that Duncan remembered. He'd reached out to her, wanting to talk, but she'd pushed him away. He'd shouted, she'd cried, and that was the end of the letters.

By the time Gran and Grandpa stopped talking, I was wrung out and came upstairs. Gran had returned my diary with a thank-you note, and left a surprise — a framed portrait of Mum, taken when she was about the same age as me.

I don't understand how her parents could have been so mean to her when they're so kind to others. Maybe the volunteering is their way of making amends. I don't know. Maybe I'll never understand. Maybe it doesn't matter.

Later

Some good news (maybe)! Grandpa heard that a hospital ship will drop anchor in the harbour on Wednesday, and on Thursday it will dock at Pier 2. So Luke could be here in *four days!*

Sunday, January 6

Went to another special service, this time at All Saints Cathedral. All the churches are having a special service today because King George proclaimed January 6 to be a Day of Prayer throughout the entire British Empire. The prayers are for the success of the Allies in the Great War.

Sometimes I forget there's a war *over there.* It feels as though it's been here.

The lieutenant-governor was at the All Saints service, as well as army and navy officers, soldiers from the garrison, sailors from the warships in port, and throngs of ordinary people.

A military band played the hymns. One of them was Dad's favourite: Oh, God, Our Help in Ages Past. I couldn't sing out loud for the ache inside, but the words were in my head. *Our shelter from the stormy blast . . .*

We told Gran that Mum had wanted us to start confirmation classes this year, but how could we with St. Mark's destroyed? She said we could choose between All Saints and St. Paul's. We chose St. Paul's because that's where the Kesslers go.

Later

Tea at the Kesslers' this afternoon.

Grandpa drove us all in his motor car. It was Duncan's first ride in one, and he was excited. I told him about my first ride, when the soldiers took me to the hospital. Today's ride was much nicer.

It was fun seeing everyone again. Crackers squawked "hellos" and Snowball curled up on my lap and purred. Sophie and Lewis drew pictures of motor cars with Duncan.

I've been thinking about Haggarty. Next time I see him I'll tell him that I now know the real story about Mum and Dad, and why Mum never talked about her parents. I like my make-believe story better. It's a bit like Romeo and Juliet. Except with a happier ending, because at least Mum and Dad had twenty-two years together. And I'm sure they loved each other right until the end.

I'd tell Gran and Grandpa they were wrong about Mum making a mistake, but I think they already know.

Monday, January 7

Eva is back!

They'd gone to Montreal, spent one night with Mr. Heine's sister, and decided it wasn't for them. So here they are in Halifax, living with Mrs. Heine's cousin until they can get a place of their own.

At first I thought I was seeing things. Duncan and I were in town with Gran, shopping for new winter coats, and I said, "Look, Duncan! Isn't that Eva?"

Sure enough it was, and not just Eva, but Werner, too!

Gran said we could spend the afternoon with our friends and leave the shopping until tomorrow. And if we wanted, we could go to the vaudeville show at the Strand Theatre. Her treat!

Duncan and Werner decided to go to Camp Hill Hospital to visit Carl, but Eva and I went off to the Strand. It was a swell show, with singing, comedy sketches and acrobats, but our favourite part was "Howard, the crayon-writing artist." He claims to have a double brain, because he can write with each hand, on a different topic, at the same time. Not only that, he does it to music! And not only forward, but backwards, upside down, topsy-turvy and in six different colours.

I tried it myself when I got home, and Duncan did, too. The double-handed forward writing wasn't so bad, but the rest? Hopeless! We obviously don't have a double brain.

I wish the regular schools would reopen. If they don't hurry up, I'll never finish the fourth reader and get on to the fifth. Even the South End schools are closed, mostly because of the broken windows, but some of them, like the Halifax Ladies College, are being used as hospitals.

Duncan says the longer it takes, the better. He's making another book about a motor car.

Almost forgot. Brian is in the same ward as Carl now. Little by little we're discovering what happened to our classmates. Most of the time the news is desperate sad.

Tuesday, January 8

This morning a letter came from Luke, but in a roundabout way — first to the Halifax Relief Committee, then to the children's committee and finally to our house. Luke says his request for compassionate leave was granted on December 17 (the same day he wrote the letter), and as soon as a ship was available, he'd be on his way home.

Of course we knew that already because of the telegram that came, but it's good to hear it again!

He's still not fit for "active duty," but he's able to get around on crutches and his bronchitis is much better. By the time he crosses the Atlantic, he says he may have "graduated" to a cane.

When I unfolded the letter and read "Dear Charlotte," I realized that Luke doesn't know that Duncan is alive. How could he? I wrote to him on December 18, before I knew myself — at least, not for certain. Luke will be some surprise!

In the afternoon I went shopping with Gran and got a new winter coat. It's royal blue with black fur trim on the collar, cuffs and pockets, and it buttons right up to the throat to keep the snow from falling down my neck. Can't wear it coasting. It's my Sunday best.

The last of the unidentified dead were buried

today and Chebucto Morgue closed down — I hope for good.

Wednesday, January 9

Went down to the harbour this morning and saw the hospital ship Grandpa mentioned. It's the first ship to be able to land in Halifax since the Explosion. Lucky for Luke, whether he's on the ship or not, because now he won't have to land in Saint John and come the rest of the way by train.

Duncan and I helped Ellie get the spare bedroom ready, because even if Luke's not here tomorrow, he'll be here eventually. Mary's getting ready, too. She asked what we thought he'd like for supper and Duncan said, "Anything but bully beef and hard biscuit."

We're desperate with hope, praying that Luke's on the ship. It's a long wait until tomorrow. And if he's *not* on board, how much longer until the next ship comes in?

Snow flurries today, and colder than yesterday.

Thursday, January 10

3:00 p.m.

Luke's home!

My heart is bursting with relief and gladness, but I'm aching sad for him. He knew about Mum, Dad and Edith, but not Ruth, and not Jane, and it fell upon me to tell him — though I waited until he was settled in at home. His loss, and the shock of seeing the devastation — all this, all at once, and meeting the grandparents for the first time, and him being exhausted from the war and the long seasick voyage. He's been asleep for the last two hours.

We were down at the pier first thing this morning. It took a good while to spot him, what with the hundreds of soldiers getting off, nearly all of them wounded, some being carried on stretchers, others barely able to walk, and finally, there he was — walking, but with a cane — just as he had hoped.

The minute we saw him, Duncan and I jumped up and down, waving and calling his name, and when he reached us on the pier he dropped his cane and kit bag and wrapped us up in his arms.

"Duncan," he says, his voice breaking, "I didn't know, I didn't dare hope, and Charlotte, thank

178

God you're still together . . . " and more of the same, and I've kept every word.

Then he steps back, puts on a worried look and says, "Are you really Charlotte and Duncan? You were little kids the last time I saw you."

"Not *that* little," says Duncan. "We were ten."

"And now you're sixteen and growing a moustache!"

"No I'm not!"

"And Charlotte here, fending off the beaux, deciding who she'll marry — "

"NO!!"

Well on it went, the bantering. I was glad of it, even though Luke might have been trying extra hard, because it took our minds off the sadness, Luke acting the way we remembered. I'd been afraid that the war might have changed him into someone different. And when he saw Kirsty! Another happy surprise, for he'd already left England by the time my letter arrived.

As soon as he wakes up I'm going to give him my diary. He can keep it as long as he likes, if he doesn't feel up to reading it right away.

I have to remind him *not* to read the parts marked "secret." I can't remember having any, but just in case.

That's all for now. I hear him talking to Duncan.

9:00 p.m.

Luke has just brought back my diary. He came into my room, drew me onto his lap and said, "I'm proud of you, Charlotte the Fearless. Thank you for keeping the family . . . " He couldn't finish, his lower lip was trembling so.

His words brought on a flood of tears, and he rocked me in his arms to comfort me. I'm too old for that, but it was good to feel like a little girl again.

But that scoundrel! I asked when I could read his diary, because that was our deal, and he said, "I've got a confession to make."

He fetched it from his room and when I opened it — blank pages! He hadn't written a single word.

"I meant to keep a diary," he says, "but ended up writing letters instead."

I don't care, now that he's home. Reading about life in the trenches might be too gruesome anyway.

He's given me his diary to use when this one is finished.

Friday, January 11

Grandpa drove us all to the Fairview Cemetery.

We brushed snow off the graves of our parents and sisters and laid wreaths of evergreens. Then we said a few prayers for Mum, Dad, Edith and Ruth. It's a comfort to know they're together, at least, and not unidentified or lost.

After that, Luke laid a wreath on Jane's grave. He'd gone to see her parents yesterday, and they'd told him where to find it.

Poor Luke. He was awfully quiet when we came back from the cemetery, but later on, Duncan mentioned how happy Jane had been when we saw her on the trolley, and how she'd shown us Luke's letter.

"You didn't read it, did you?" Luke says, with a worried look.

We pretended we had, to tease *him* for a change, making up one gushy sentence after another, but eventually admitted we were fooling.

He'd read about Jane in my diary, but wanted to hear it all again. What she was wearing, what she said and so on. I think it cheered him a little.

I don't need to write every day, not with Luke being here, but sometimes I get the urge to write anyway. This sooty old diary is still a comfort, although the biggest comfort is Luke.

Duncan and I are like two puppies, the way we follow him around. It's a wonder we don't howl when he's out of our sight. We take turns sitting beside him at meals and hang on to his every word. We go on walks with him no matter what the weather, making sure he goes slowly and uses his cane, reminding him every ten seconds to watch his step, until he finally says, "You two are worse than a sergeant for bellowing orders!" And we say, "Well then, we'll let you fall and break the other leg so you'll be stuck with us for good!"

The last few days have been right holy miserable. Damp sticky snow, up to our ankles in puddles with the wind whipping around the corners. And Luke? Stay indoors with his feet up? No, he's loving it because "it's not the blasted trenches." And what an appetite! He's sure been missing good food over there. Gosh, the way he devours Mary's cooking! And no sooner has he finished a meal than he's in the kitchen looking for a snack. Mary acts mad and threatens him with her rolling pin, but eventually gives in. Then she gives Duncan and me a snack, too, because she doesn't "play favourites."

Sometimes Luke asks Ellie to slip him a little extra when she's serving, but she just laughs and says, "You don't need *my* help, the way you've wormed your way into Mary's heart!"

Duncan wanted to know about Vimy and Passchendaele, but Luke won't talk about the battles. "You've seen enough horror," he says. "You don't need to hear any more."

He showed us the army way of polishing brass buttons, and made us laugh with his tales of training fleas to do tricks, and how pet lice were the latest rage because once you had one, you'd never be without.

We laughed ourselves silly when he talked about a show that his battalion put on, how he'd dressed up as a mademoiselle in a flouncy skirt, red lipstick and a curly blond wig, playing the part of a waitress in a French tavern. "You desire the billy beef, Monsieur?"

Luke keeps things light-hearted, and doesn't say much about the Explosion. I know he's hurting, though, because sometimes at night I hear him weeping.

We talk a lot about the way things were before. Our house with the stained glass window, Mum's good cooking and how she tried to fatten me up,

Dad and his poetry recitations, Ruth's temper, Edith's long line of beaux.

It was hard at first, talking about them, but it's gotten a bit easier, and it's a way of having them close. The memories make us cry. But sometimes, the things we remember, we can't help but laugh. Like the time Edith and Ruth set up a pet hospital in the backyard, and everything was fine until people started looking for their lost cats and kittens, and Mum complained about the amount of food disappearing from the kitchen.

And the day Dad came home with a big box and told Luke to open it — no one knew what was inside, not even Mum — and there was dear little Kirsty. Everyone gasped and went "Ahh!" Oh, the fun we had when she was a puppy.

Gran and Grandpa listen, too. Sometimes they laugh and say, "Just like your mother at that age." Then they tell us something they've remembered. Like when Mum forged her mother's handwriting and wrote a letter to her teacher asking that Lily be excused from all physical activities because of growing pains. It sounds like the very thing Ruth would do.

Friday, January 18

Grandpa told us that we can "file a claim" and get paid for the loss of our house and all its contents. So Luke, Duncan and I sat down and made a list. We went through the house, room by room, item by item, trying to picture everything in our minds. It took a long time because the smallest item brought back memories. Mum's embroidery on the pillow slips, the squeaky clothes wringer, the dinner dishes with yellow roses (used only on Sundays and special occasions). Furniture, carpet in the living room, lino in the kitchen — so much a part of our home but scarcely noticed.

So much to think about. And questions. Does the stained glass window count? Yes, all the windows. What about the piano? No, a piano is a luxury.

We had to list our clothing, right down to stockings and underwear, and after that, the cost of everything. Sofa, lamps, tea kettle, rolling pin, every last little thing . . .

By the time Duncan and I finished our clothing list, we'd had enough. We left the pricing to the others.

Later, I noticed that the blue velveteen dress Edith had been making me for Christmas had been added to my list. Gran must have remembered it from my diary.

Miss Tebo was killed in the explosion, so today I started piano lessons with a new teacher, Miss Chatwin. She's nice and doesn't rap knuckles. (I know because I didn't see a ruler.) She gave me lots to work on and said I might be ready for the conservatory exam in the spring if I practise hard.

Later on, Luke, Duncan and I went to Camp Hill Hospital. Most of the Explosion patients have left and the beds have gone back to the soldiers. Luke wanted to see some friends who were injured in France.

Duncan and I went to a different ward to see Carl. He was playing cards with three of the soldier patients and won the game just as we arrived, so he was in good spirits. His broken leg is on the mend and he's leaving the hospital at the end of the month.

Brian left the hospital a week ago. He and his family are moving to Boston.

And as we were leaving the hospital we met Helen! I introduced her to my brothers, and when she and Luke were shaking hands and chatting, Duncan whispered, "Charlotte the Matchmaker."

Gosh, I hope Helen didn't hear him.

Sunday, January 20

St. Paul's in the morning.

Rev. LeMoine was there. He told us that the Methodists and Presbyterians of Richmond are raising funds to build a temporary church, and everyone from Richmond, no matter what their faith, will be able to attend while waiting for their own churches to be rebuilt.

Luke wanted to see what's happening in Richmond so, in the afternoon, we went to a spot just outside the devastated area. Luke's astonished by the amount of work going on, and even more astonished by what's already been done. Especially considering the harsh winter. Horses, wagons, workmen everywhere, great piles of wood and bricks and tarpaper, ruins cleared away, roads put in, houses that weren't destroyed being repaired. Like the Chisholms' house, where the repairs are almost finished. A roofer told us that in another week the family will be able to move back in. I'll be glad to see Muriel again.

Practised the piano for two hours before supper. I'm determined to take the conservatory exam.

Monday, January 21

Bad news. Luke has to go back to France. His ship sails in three weeks. He was given leave partly because of his leg, but he's seen an army doctor who said he was fit to return. I wish he had fallen and broken his other leg.

He might have been able to stay on compassionate leave, if Duncan and I didn't have relatives to take care of us, but we do. I hate the army and its rules. I hate the war.

To cheer us up, Luke sang some of the verses to "Mademoiselle from Armentières" that his brigade made up. Here's my favourite. I'm spelling the words the way the soldiers do, even though it's not proper French.

Mademoiselle from Armentières, parley-voo?
Mademoiselle from Armentières, parley-voo?
She had three chins, her knees would knock,
Her face would stop a cuckoo clock.
Hinky-dinky, parley-voo.

There's another verse that says the officers get the wine and steak, but "all we get is a bellyache."

Almost forgot the good news. Grandpa says the Maine Military Hospital is closing down, so the building can go back to being the Halifax Ladies College. That's where I might be going.

Tuesday, January 22

Bedtime

Some days, just one little thing . . . like this morning in town, a greeting card with the words *To a Dear Mother* . . .

Saturday, February 2

Groundhog Day. Sunny from dawn till dusk, so the groundhog for sure saw his shadow. Six more weeks of this terrible winter.

Haven't written in my diary for almost two weeks, with Luke being here. The best news is that Muriel and her family have moved back to Richmond. Muriel and I were planning to go coasting on Monday but couldn't because of the weather.

All week it's been stormy and cold. Some nights I haven't been able to sleep, with the wind shrieking and branches scratching against the windows. Kirsty's allowed to sleep with me now, but she's as nervous as I am. Every loud thump or bang makes us jump.

I've spent most of my time indoors, except for going to church and piano lessons. I read books from Grandpa's library, play cards and checkers with Luke or Duncan, work on the hooked rug I started last week, and practise practise practise.

I'm knitting again. Gran's teaching me to do a cable stitch so I can knit myself a fancy tuque. And Luke better not tease me about it! He's always wearing the scarf I knitted for him last Christmas, but before he puts it on it's, "Gosh, Charlotte. It's a foot longer than it was yesterday." Well I know it's stretching, but not that much.

Grandpa's teaching Duncan to play chess, and Luke's learning to play the fiddle. I never knew Grandpa had a fiddle until he brought it over to the piano one afternoon, tuned it up, and started playing along with me.

Yesterday the mercury dropped way below zero. Another day indoors except for Luke. He braved the cold to have tea at Helen's!

Last night Duncan had a nightmare, the first since Luke's been home. I couldn't understand the words but he was crying out in a panic.

I went to his room and we ended up playing checkers. Then Luke came in because he couldn't sleep either. Duncan showed him the picture he'd drawn of Luke dressed up as a waitress in a French tavern. Luke said there was nothing better than going into a tavern in Armentières and having a real meal for a change. He pronounced *Ar-*

mentières the proper French way and said, "You can bet Mum's listening."

Then we talked about our family, and the things they'd most like to hear us say. Luke recited the first verse of Dad's favourite poem, "The Cremation of Sam McGee": *"There are strange things done in the midnight sun . . . "*

He sounded so like Dad.

We agreed that Ruth would like us to say what a fine actress she was, a star in the making, the next Mary Pickford.

And Edith? "She was pretty and talented as well as kind," Luke said. "But you could never pay her a compliment. She'd only blush and say, 'Oh, go on.'"

"She was the best sister in the world and I loved her," I said. I hope she was listening, because I never thought to tell her when I had the chance.

We talked about how lucky Luke has been in France, so far — but didn't say too much, in case we were tempting fate. Duncan reminded us of something Dad used to say. "If it was raining soup, we'd all have forks and knives, and Luke would be the one with the spoon."

Gran took me to town to buy my Halifax Ladies College uniform.

I wish classes were starting tomorrow, but I have to wait until March.

Eva came over in the afternoon. She wishes she could go to H.L.C., but she's going to Tower Road School.

We had tea with Gran, and Luke joined us for a while, Eva blushing whenever Luke gave a nod in her direction. He's such a charmer. He can even make Gran blush!

After tea I took Eva to my room and showed her the tuque I'm knitting, not the one for me but a secret one for Luke, and told her how he's been teasing me about the scarf. She suggested we make up a limerick for when he goes overseas. Well the first two lines were easy, but after that we were stumped. There was no end of giggles as we tried different rhymes, like *fluke, duke, puke.* After that we tried words that would rhyme if you had a Scottish accent, like *book, brook, crook.* It was good fun, and when we'd decided on a limerick we wrote it on a card to give to Luke.

Here it is:

There once was a fellow named Luke,
Whose sister knitted a tuque.

It was meant for his head
But unravelled instead
So away with a cold went poor Luke.

Before I could stop her, Eva added another line: *And by hook or by crook, that'll teach him to tease his sister.*

What a scamp!

Not only that, but as she was leaving she says, "Luke is so handsome!"

"Go on, he's just my brother." I shrugged it off, trying to sound like Edith, but inside I was proud.

Six more days until he leaves. "No tears," he says, "It only makes it harder." So for his sake, I put on a brave face and smile, and do my crying when I'm alone in my room. Like now.

Thursday, February 7

Not so cold today, so went coasting with Muriel and Eva.

After that we walked to the South Commons to visit Muriel's Uncle Jim and Auntie Belle. They're renting one of the new apartments, but only until the permanent houses are built. Then they'll move into one of those. They got to pick out their own furniture, sent free all the way from Massachusetts.

Uncle Jim says there's a thousand people from

Richmond in the apartments, and everyone's mixed up, Anglicans living next door to Catholics and so on. Muriel says the Richmond schools won't be opening for a long time. She says it's too bad I don't live there anymore, because of the long holiday, but I told her I can't wait to go to school.

She says, "You'll hate Halifax Ladies College. The girls are uppity snobs."

Oh, Muriel, the same as ever.

It was fun seeing her little cousins again. They were some excited to see Kirsty.

One more thing. Luke took Helen on a sleigh ride that lasted the whole afternoon. I never planned to be a matchmaker, but I turned out to be a good one. Luke seems to be quite smitten.

Four days until he leaves.

Sunday, February 10

Duncan and I were helping Luke pack up his kit, teasing him about Helen and so on, but when they started singing "Mademoiselle from Armentières" I thought of Mum, and the Explosion, and Luke going away, and I couldn't bear it. I had to run into my room to keep from crying.

I feel a bit better now. Gran came in a while ago. She took me in her arms and said it's all right to cry, so cry I did, great heaving sobs, until I was spent.

Now I'm going downstairs to help Gran fill a tin with the treats Mary baked yesterday. Luke will be able to eat them on the ship if he doesn't get seasick.

Later

Luke has given me all the letters our family wrote to him, starting from the day he first went overseas. "Why leave them with me?" I asked, and he said, "You're the keeper of the family stories."

I felt honoured, but desperate sad.

At church this morning I prayed that his luck will run out and he'll be wounded in France. Not a serious wound, but bad enough to put him in the hospital like before. Only this time, he'd have to *stay* there until the war is over.

Now I'm praying that God will ignore that prayer, because even a little wound could become deadly. What was I thinking? Luke recovered from his injuries once, but he may not be so lucky a second time.

Monday, February 11

Everyone went to see Luke off, even Kirsty.

We'd all taken little gifts, like gum, hard candies, a deck of playing cards, Duncan's drawings, the limerick verse and so on. There was no time to be sad because we kept taking things out of our pockets and pretending to be surprised, as if we hadn't put the gifts in ourselves. "Well, what have we here?" Grandpa would say, showing a pack of cigarettes. "Must be for Luke." Then someone else would do the same, and so on.

It was fun, because Luke then had to find a place to put everything! His kit bag was already bulging, so he ended up stuffing his pockets, and when they were full, he wrapped the rest of the gifts in his scarf. "Plenty of room in here," he says, teasing me till the end.

In the middle of all this, Helen arrived! So untie the scarf, add Helen's little gifts, and tie up the scarf again. By then it was time for him to go.

Sunday, March 3

Three weeks since my last entry.

I was in low spirits after Luke went away, lost and empty feeling. Didn't want to write in my diary, or do much of anything. Duncan was low, too, and we spent long hours talking, or just being quiet together.

Then we got over the blues, and wrote a long letter to Luke. We made it funny, as if it were written by Kirsty, and said things about Charlotte and Duncan and the rest of the household, but from a dog's point of view. Everyone laughed when we read it out loud, and we're going to write more letters that way. We take turns writing paragraphs.

Last week we spent a day at Haggarty's farm. It was some good to visit him and see how well he's coming along with the one eye. He and Mrs. Haggarty told us what they could about our Richmond neighbours, and the people I knew from the milk run. We told them about Luke and our grandparents.

I'm so thankful for Gran, the way she's always ready to sit with me over a cup of tea and listen while I pour my heart out. I'm able to talk to her in a way I never could with Mum.

Well it's about time I got back to my regular habit of writing every day, especially now. Why? Because tomorrow's my first day at Halifax Ladies College!

I'm too excited to write any more.

Monday, March 4

A long wait till breakfast, but I'm already dressed and ready for school. Woke up a couple of times in the night, but the minute I started to feel anxious I heard Sophie's little voice saying, "You're Charlotte the Fearless. You can do anything."

4:45 p.m.

I'm home! Just a few lines, and then I'll start my homework.

It felt good being back in a classroom. We even had a composition to write. The topic was winter. I wrote as my title "A Symphony of Winter," and made winter a wonderland of "glistening icicles" and "feathery soft snow." Not a bit like this cruel winter.

Gran walked with me this morning, and the first thing I saw in the foyer was a plaque with my mother's name. *Lillian Wakefield. Student of the Year, 1895.* The year she graduated.

It made me proud, but nervous, the thought of following in Mum's footsteps and not disappointing her or Gran.

The Charlotte I used to be could never have

imagined herself in a new school in a new area, not one familiar face, and her own face marked with a ragged blue scar. But I'm not the same Charlotte.

Did I shy away brooding or hide my face in a book? No, I walked up to the girls in my class and asked them questions about the school, teachers, lessons and so on. I told them that if they wanted to know what happened to me in the Explosion, they could come right out and ask instead of whispering and pitying behind my back. I said I didn't mind if they stared at my scar. (A few girls were doing just that, when they thought I wasn't looking.) Because why should I be ashamed or embarrassed? It's a sign of survival.

Saturday, March 9

Went to the Kesslers' today. Took Kirsty for a walk with Sophie. Came back and watched Duncan and Lewis run the electric train. After that we went to the Home for Children to see Matthew and Kevin. They're going to Tower Road School in a couple of weeks, same as Duncan. I felt left out with all the talk of Tower Road. That's where Eva's going, too. Came back through town so Duncan could buy a new harmonica.

Wednesday, March 13

Sometimes I go for a whole day, even two days, without remembering, but all at once it hits me. Like today. I was walking home from school and heard a man whistling, "Pack Up Your Troubles," just like Dad.

I cried all the way home.

Friday, March 15

Today I heard a happy sound. Duncan playing his harmonica.

Sunday, March 17

Went to Richmond with Duncan for the first service in the "tarpaper" church. It's the one Rev. LeMoine told us was being built. Right now it's for people of all faiths: Methodists, Presbyterians, Catholics and Anglicans.

It was hard at first, being there. A gathering of survivors, in a Richmond that's no longer Richmond, where a scarred or bandaged face is common and where the absent faces fill your mind and heart at every turn.

It wasn't a service of mourning, though. It was

more a celebration of being together and looking to the future.

And the weather felt like spring, a new beginning.

Later

A weight has been lifted, a weight I never realized I was carrying until now. I've changed my mind about going to Halifax Ladies College. I liked the school, and the girls didn't seem uppity, but somehow, it didn't feel right. I've decided to go to Tower Road School instead.

Gran said it's a wise decision as I'm bound to feel more comfortable there, with children I know. She assured me she wasn't disappointed (I was afraid she might be) and I shouldn't feel pressured about H.LC. just because it was Mum's school. Besides, I can always go back when I'm older.

I'm happy and excited about going to Tower Road, especially since Eva and Duncan will be there. What was I thinking, going to a school without Duncan? No wonder it didn't feel right. The "Intrepidous Twins" have to stay together.

Thursday, March 21

The calendar says it's the first day of spring, but whoever decided that never knew Halifax. It's gone back to being cold and windy and the ground is still covered with snow.

But never mind the weather. Miss Chatwin's holding a spring concert at the end of April, for her conservatory pupils, and I'm playing a piano solo! I haven't decided what to play.

Sunday, March 24

7:00 p.m.

This is my last entry.

I've been thinking about my diary and the story it tells, not from the words but from the state of the pages. At the very beginning, a few blotches of mud from the trenches in France. Then nine weeks or so of crisp, buff-coloured pages marching along in an orderly way, one day at a time. For a month after that, the pages are streaked with tears and horribly marked with blood and soot. Little by little they begin to clear up, and in the last few entries, the pages are clean. But the cover is scarred, like me.

One day, when I reread the first part of my

diary, I'll see my family again and hear their voices. Mum, Dad, Edith and Ruth. I'll also see a
younger Charlotte Blackburn.

I don't want to go back to the self I was then,
wondering about questions that have no answers,
worrying about things that don't matter. Like it
says in the "Pack Up Your Troubles" song, *"What's
the use of worrying?"*

The other day, Gran asked what I want to be
when I grow up, before I become a wife and
mother. I told her I didn't know because I don't
think that far ahead anymore. I just want be a
good person and make the most out of every single day.

Oh! I've just decided! I'm going to play the
Chopin waltz for the recital, the one that Edith
used to play. Everyone in our family loved it. I'm
sure they'll all be listening.

Carpe diem. Time to start practising.

Epilogue

Overseas, the war news was grim. A string of German victories in the spring of 1918 made Charlotte more fearful than ever that Luke might not return safely, but she kept her worries to herself. Nor did she express them in the diary he'd left for her. She was saving that diary for when the war was finally over.

She wrote long, breezy letters to Luke, recounting the small events at home and at school in as lighthearted a way as possible, so he wouldn't worry about her and Duncan.

By the end of April 1918, Charlotte was well into the daily routine of home and school, and happy with her decision to attend Tower Road with Duncan and Eva. She knew several other children from the old Richmond neighbourhood, and made new friends among the South End girls.

It was during this time, when life was seemingly getting back to "normal," that the full impact of Charlotte's loss hit home. In the days following the Explosion there had been such an overwhelming amount to bear, it was as if her mind had gone numb. She often wondered how she would have coped had it not been for Duncan and, later on, her grandparents and Luke.

"You're Charlotte the Fearless," Duncan would remind her. "You would have managed."

She found it helpful to talk to someone during her worst bouts of sadness, and found sympathetic listeners in Gran and Eva. Duncan, while sharing and understanding Charlotte's grief, continued to suffer from recurring nightmares and steadfastly refused to talk about his experience during the Explosion. They supported each other through the difficult times, although Charlotte was the one who most often eased Duncan's worries, rather than the other way around — a pattern which would continue for many years.

Luke wrote as often as possible after his return overseas, but when six weeks went by without a word, the twins began to suspect the worst.

Finally, near the end of May, they received a letter from a convalescent hospital in England. Several weeks earlier, while in France, Luke had developed acute bronchial pneumonia. He would be returning to Halifax on a hospital ship and continuing his convalescence at Camp Hill Hospital.

It was the very thing Charlotte had prayed for — as long as Luke's condition didn't get worse.

"Luke the Lucky," she said, on her first visit to the hospital. She reminded him of their father's quip about "raining soup," and hid her concern over his frail appearance. Later, as he began to recover more fully, she teased him about losing weight on purpose so that Mary would have even more fun fattening him up.

By the end of September he was well enough to leave the hospital. A good thing, too, for by then the world was fighting a new and deadly enemy — Spanish influenza. The epidemic reached Canada in mid-September and, by early October, it was raging in Halifax. Schools, churches and businesses were closed, all public meetings were cancelled, and people were advised to stay indoors. By the time the epidemic had run its course, it had taken the lives of some fifty thousand Canadians.

Charlotte, her brothers and grandparents held a quiet celebration on November 11, the day the Great War ended, and she started her new diary that evening. "A new beginning," she wrote. "I am determined to take Mum's advice to seize the day, and I am taking hold of this historic day, November 11, 1918, with thanksgiving — thankful that the war is over, that Luke, Duncan and I have survived, and that we have found a loving home in the most unexpected of places."

The year she turned fifteen, Charlotte left Tower Road School and attended the Halifax Ladies College, where she graduated in 1923.

The Halifax Relief Commission provided pensions for victims of the Explosion, and orphans who had lost both parents were entitled to receive a monthly allowance of sixteen dollars, payable until their seventeenth birthday. Charlotte's grandparents had encouraged her and Duncan to save their allowances to further their education, and promised they would provide whatever additional funds were needed.

Charlotte would never know why her life had been spared, but she vowed that it would not be wasted. In the fall of 1923 she enrolled in Dalhousie University to study medicine.

It was an unusual choice for a woman, but not unheard of, and certainly not impossible for one as determined as Charlotte.

Besides, things were changing in the world. The Roaring Twenties, as the decade came to be called, was an exciting time, marked by a break with traditions and the feeling that the world was on the brink of a different era. Listening to the radio was a popular craze in the Twenties. Radios had become affordable, and the new, innovative sound of jazz was hitting the airwaves. Along with jazz, a new dance called the Charleston was spreading in popularity. Whenever possible, Charlotte would abandon her studies, coax Eva or Duncan into doing the same, and go off to kick up her heels. It was at a New Year's Eve dance in 1928 that she met the man who would eventually become her husband — Rory MacPherson, a trumpet player in a dance band.

The fun of dancing and listening to jazz served as a much-needed respite after the horrors of the Great War and the Explosion, even though such horrors were still present in everyone's mind. Charlotte never "got over" her loss. The pain softened over time, but certain occasions, such as Christmas, were always tinged with sadness.

For many years, Charlotte worked as a family physician in Halifax. She continued to live in her grandparents' house following their deaths, and insisted that Mary stay on as cook and housekeeper for as long as she liked. By now Charlotte was used to Mary's scolding about not eating enough, and secretly enjoyed being spoiled. Her two Brittany spaniels had their share of spoiling, too.

Duncan became an Anglican minister and served in several small parishes in Shelbourne County, the area where his father grew up. When the Second World War broke out in September 1939, he went overseas as an army chaplain. He returned to Halifax four years later with an English bride, and settled in the South End, not far from Young Avenue. They had one son.

Luke became a history teacher. His romance with Helen ended soon after the war, and in 1921 he married a young teacher from Truro. They settled in one of the new hydrostone houses in Richmond, where they raised four children.

Charlotte kept up with her piano playing, both classical and jazz, and often performed at concerts. In the spring of 1936, at a fundraising concert for the Children's Orphanage, she was reacquainted with trumpeter Rory MacPherson, now teaching music at Dalhousie. They were married the following year and had one daughter, Lily.

Many of the survivors Charlotte had known in her childhood moved away following the Explosion and never returned to Halifax. She kept in touch with as many as possible, and remained lifelong friends with those who stayed. Haggarty, Muriel, Eva, Carl — they and their families were among the many visitors to the house on Young Avenue, where Charlotte continued to live as a wife and mother.

Those who had opened their homes and their hearts in the aftermath of the Explosion were not forgotten, either. Helen, who married before completing her medical studies, became a close friend of the family, as did the Kesslers.

Throughout their lives, Charlotte and Duncan

remained best friends. For those who knew them well, it was no surprise that Charlotte died just two months after her brother, at the age of eighty-eight.

The extended families of Charlotte, Duncan and Luke continued the tradition of attending the memorial service held on Fort Needham, every December 6 at 9:05 a.m.

One more thing (as Charlotte would say). As Lily was going through her mother's belongings, she found several diaries, including one old and weathered diary written at the time of the Explosion. She kept it for many years, and eventually donated it to her local library.

She also found a dozen letters marked *Return to Sender.* They had been opened and read many times, judging by the well-thumbed pages, and Lily lost no time in reading them herself. Knowing the family history, she discovered no trace of anger, bitterness or regret in her grandmother's letters. They merely recorded, often with humour, always with love and pride, small moments in the life of the growing Blackburn family.

Historical Note

Thursday, December 6, 1917, dawned crisp and clear in Halifax, Nova Scotia. It began like most days during the Great War, with Haligonians following their regular routines. It would end like no other.

The war had made Halifax one of the busiest and most prosperous ports in the British Empire. Most troops heading for Europe passed through its harbour, as well as enormous quantities of supplies — horses, foodstuffs, hospital supplies, munitions, and tons of grain and lumber. The dry dock echoed with the building and repairing of ships. Piers, barges, freighters, foundries and factories were scenes of constant activity.

It wasn't the first time that Halifax had prospered in war. From the moment the British discovered the huge natural harbour that breaks into the Atlantic coast of Nova Scotia, the strategic importance of the site was recognized. Halifax would be built as a military fortress and naval base on the western side of the harbour, a perfect place for the British to uphold their interests in North America and to offset the French stronghold in Louisbourg, Cape Breton.

The choice was ideal, as the harbour is one of

the finest in the world. It's shaped roughly like an hourglass. One end is the landlocked Bedford Basin, an inner harbour where over thirty vessels can lie in safety. The other end, open to the sea, is the harbour itself. Connecting the two is a narrow passage known as the Narrows.

Halifax was first settled in 1749. By 1917 its population had risen to fifty thousand, ten times that of Dartmouth, its neighbour across the harbour. Who could have foreseen that the city, prospering from the war, would soon know devastation beyond anyone's imagination?

When war broke out in August 1914, young men eighteen and older enlisted with boundless enthusiasm. Off to the battlefields, give the Germans a pounding, and be home for Christmas, they thought — the adventure of a lifetime. The reality was something else.

From the very beginning, Canada and other Allies (supporters of Britain) suffered heavy losses. Hospital ships carrying wounded men arrived in Halifax regularly. Before long, the number of volunteers enlisting in the Canadian army fell behind the increasing number of casualties. In an effort to solve this problem, the Canadian government under Prime Minister Robert Borden passed the Military Service Act, to bring about what was known as conscription. Under this law, all unmarried men aged twenty to thirty-four were required to register for military service, unless they could claim an exemption.

The losses were not only heavy, but costly. The Allies were losing so many ships to German submarines, they began crossing the Atlantic in convoys, escorted by heavily armed destroyers.

By late 1917 the situation in Europe was desperate. Munitions were in such great demand that cargo ships of every description were pressed into service — no matter how old or battered. One such ship was a French steamer called *Mont-Blanc*.

Mont-Blanc was a floating bomb. She carried 2,300 tons of wet and dry picric acid, 200 tons of TNT, 10 tons of gun cotton and 35 tons of benzol (a high-octane gasoline), which was stored in iron drums and placed on the open deck. The steamer also carried guns for defence and more than 300 live rounds of ammunition.

By all accounts, the cargo was stowed with every possible precaution. Dockworkers loading the ship in New York were required to cover their metal-studded boots with cloth, since one spark could set off an explosion. And since matches were strictly forbidden on deck, the crew resorted to using chewing tobacco instead of smoking cigarettes.

The *Mont-Blanc's* Captain LeMedec had never

intended to sail to Halifax before crossing the Atlantic. He and his forty-one man crew had expected to travel in a convoy from New York. But his ship was rejected for being too slow, and he was ordered to proceed to Halifax and join a convoy there.

The ill-fated journey began on the night of December 1. *Mont-Blanc* left New York on her own. Her arrival in Halifax was delayed by a gale, but late Wednesday afternoon, December 5, she arrived at the mouth of Halifax Harbour.

Regular procedures were followed. Local pilot Francis Mackey boarded the ship and directed her to the nearby examination boat for inspection. The examining officer boarded to interview Captain LeMedec. He also inspected the ship's cargo manifest, which listed the explosives.

Mont-Blanc passed inspection, but she was unable to enter the harbour. Not because of the dangerous cargo she carried, but because she had arrived too late to pass through the anti-submarine nets.

Halifax Harbour was protected by two such nets, an outer one and an inner one. Each net consisted of steel wire netting suspended from the surface of the water to the harbour bottom, and was held up by a long line of wooden floats. A "gate" in the net's mid-section could be opened by the two civilian tugboats assigned to act as "gate vessels." The outer net was kept open until an inbound ship or convoy had passed through. Once it was closed, the inner net was opened.

The nets were not opened between dusk and dawn for security reasons. So, because of *Mont-Blanc's* late arrival, she was required to anchor off shore and wait until the morning.

That same night, another ship lay in wait. *Imo* was a Norwegian-registered ship leased for Belgian Relief. Much larger and faster than *Mont-Blanc,* it had anchored in the Bedford Basin two days earlier. Her Norwegian captain had obtained permission to leave Halifax on December 5, but a coal tender had arrived later than expected. By the time it filled up *Imo's* bunkers, the anti-submarine nets were closed.

The next morning, at 7:30 a.m., *Imo* pulled up anchor and proceeded towards the Narrows. A steamer wanting to anchor on the western side of the Basin turned to the left (to port) instead of to the right (to starboard), and forced the *Imo* towards the Dartmouth shore, the wrong channel for outgoing ships. A local tugboat with two barges in tow, following in the wake of the steamer, forced *Imo* still closer to Dartmouth. Meanwhile, *Mont-Blanc* was coming into the Narrows. She signalled to *Imo* that she was in her correct channel. *Imo,* however, signalled that she was intending to continue even farther to port.

Again the *Mont-Blanc* signalled that she intended to pass to starboard, the normal rule for ships in harbours or narrow channels. By this time she was close to the Dartmouth shore. She expected *Imo* to give her room by swinging towards Halifax, but once again *Imo* signalled that she intended to stay her course.

The ships were now dangerously close. Both took emergency action. *Mont-Blanc* decided to go hard to port and changed her path diagonally towards Halifax, right across the bow of *Imo*. At the same instant, *Imo* signalled that she had reversed her engines.

The action taken by either vessel would have avoided a collision had the other ship stayed its original course. But with the reversal of her engines, *Imo*'s bow swung into the path of *Mont-Blanc* and cut a deep wedge into her starboard side. It was 8:45 a.m.

Almost at once, *Mont-Blanc* was on fire. The crew and pilot took to the lifeboats and rowed furiously to Dartmouth, leaving the abandoned ship to drift into Halifax Harbour, Pier 6, just off the community of Richmond. Before coming to a halt, the ship brushed against the pier and set it ablaze.

To the crowds gathering on both sides of the harbour, the burning ship was not a floating bomb, but a spectacle. Men, women and children rushed to windows and rooftops and hurried down to the waterfront to watch the excitement. Passengers on the Dartmouth–Halifax ferry, halfway across the Narrows at the time, watched from the decks. On every ship in the harbour, sailors and stevedores abandoned their duties. Several vessels in the harbour made for *Mont-Blanc* with fire hoses, and the Halifax Fire Department was quick to respond. They were positioning their new, motorized fire engine when *Mont-Blanc* exploded. It was a few seconds short of 9:05 a.m.

The force of the explosion blasted the 3,000-ton ship into a spray of metallic fragments. The barrel of one of her cannons landed almost 6 kilometres away, near Dartmouth. Part of her anchor shank, weighing over half a ton, landed 3 kilometres to the west of Halifax. Chunks of metal crashed through roofs, and damaged ships. Windows were shattered within a radius of 80 kilometres, and the report was heard as far away as Prince Edward Island. The shock was even felt in Sydney, Cape Breton, more than 430 kilometres northeast of Halifax.

The blast and shock waves flattened much of

the Richmond area — railway terminals, docks and residential areas — while across the harbour, damage in the less densely populated Dartmouth area was almost equally severe.

The explosion also caused a tsunami. Sweeping in as high as eighteen metres above the high-water mark on the Halifax side, and crashing against the shore on the Dartmouth side, the wave added greatly to the loss of life and property.

Over sixteen hundred people were killed instantly by the blast. Subsequent deaths caused by the tsunami or the numerous fires, or by critical injuries, brought the total close to two thousand.

Nine thousand were injured, including the hundreds who suffered eye damage or permanent blindness due to flying glass. The North End of Halifax was almost completely destroyed, leaving some twenty-five thousand people without adequate housing, and six thousand homeless.

Four residents of Africville were killed, likely while working in Richmond. The community itself, situated beyond the Narrows on the south side of Bedford Basin, suffered minor damage. The Mi'kmaq village at Tufts Cove, on the Dartmouth shore, was destroyed and never rebuilt. Nine of the twenty-one residents lost their lives.

Amazingly, the Dartmouth–Halifax ferry continued its morning run to Halifax, and kept on running throughout the day, allowing survivors to reach loved ones or to find shelter. There were no deaths among the 9:00 a.m. passengers, only minor injuries from shattered glass.

Relief efforts were rapidly set in motion. There were some five thousand soldiers in Halifax at the time, as well as sailors from the Canadian and British navies. Military medical facilities were available to provide personnel and supplies. By noon on December 6, city officials had met with army and naval commanders to organize transportation, food, shelter and rescue teams. The Halifax Relief Committee was established to oversee all aspects of the disaster, and over a dozen sub-committees quickly set about their tasks.

Response from outside the city was equally swift. Within hours of the explosion, relief trains from towns in Nova Scotia and New Brunswick were on their way, bringing surgeons, nurses and supplies. Money began to pour in from as far away as Britain, China and New Zealand. Although half a dozen hospitals were performing operations immediately after the explosion, they were scarcely able to cope with the large number of wounded. The recently opened Camp Hill Hospital, for example, designed to accommodate over two hundred convalescing soldiers, was overwhelmed with some fourteen hundred victims. Patients who were there at the time were turned out of their beds to accommodate the more urgent cases.

Shelters were desperately needed too, especially in light of the fierce blizzard that hit the city on December 7. The storm, one of the worst in the city's history, not only hampered rescue efforts, it slowed down the arrival of relief trains and repair crews. Still, by the night of December 9, telephone and telegraph repairmen had managed to restore some three hundred telephone lines, and had connected emergency lines to all the relief centres. Some of the telegraph lines were up and running the very night of the explosion.

The people of Massachusetts, particularly the citizens of Boston, gave unstintingly in volunteer medical assistance, money and goods. Since 1971, the province of Nova Scotia has sent an annual Christmas tree to Boston to show its gratitude.

In early 1918 the Dominion government appointed the Halifax Relief Commission to oversee the rebuilding of the North End and to compensate people for injuries and property loss. The program continues to help the remaining survivors.

Reconstruction took place with astounding speed. By late January 1918, three thousand repair orders had been completed and hundreds of people were able to return to their homes. Temporary apartment buildings were erected on three separate sites, and by mid-March, over three hundred apartments were ready to be occupied, complete with furnishings and household goods provided by the Massachusetts–Halifax Relief Fund.

In the fall of 1918, construction began on an extensive new development — shops, offices and houses — built from cement blocks called hydrostones. Wide streets and green spaces were incorporated into the design, and, within three years, about two thousand people were living in the "Hydrostone."

Gradually, the demolished areas in Halifax were put back together. Life went on, but nothing could compensate for the lives which had been lost. Within two months of the Explosion, over fifteen hundred victims had been buried. Many of those were unidentified. More victims were discovered in the spring. Some were never found. Hundreds of children were orphaned.

Who was to blame for the disaster?

Six days after the explosion, an inquiry opened at the Halifax courthouse. Two months later, the Justice ruled against *Mont-Blanc*, stating that the ship's captain and the local pilot were wholly responsible for the collision and, ultimately, the explosion. Both men were found guilty of neglect of public safety for not warning the city of a probable explosion. The acting commander of the Royal Canadian Navy was found guilty of neglect in performing his duty as chief examining officer. All three men were arrested and charged with manslaughter, but the charges were later dismissed because of insufficient evidence.

The owners of *Mont-Blanc* and *Imo* appealed and cross-appealed, and each party filed for damages against the other. In May 1919, the Supreme Court of Canada found the two ships equally responsible. A further appeal was made, this time to the Privy Council in London, England. In February 1920, it ultimately declared *Imo* and *Mont-Blanc* equally to blame.

As Halifax set about rebuilding, news of the Great War once again claimed the front page of local newspapers. Canadian forces, commanded by General Arthur Currie, continued to distinguish themselves with courage and determination on the battlefields of Belgium and France. In the fall of 1918, they took part in offensives that eventually crushed the retreating Germans. On November 11, Germany surrendered.

"The war to end all wars" proved to the world that Canada was an independent nation in her own right, and no longer just a part of the British

Empire. It marked Canada's "coming of age," but at a terrible price — out of some six hundred thousand Canadians who went overseas, almost one out of ten did not return.

And the Halifax Explosion? That single disaster brought the ravages of war to the heart of Halifax, causing the deaths of more Nova Scotians than were killed in four years of war. Until the dropping of the atomic bomb on Hiroshima in 1945, it was the largest man-made explosion in history.

The tragedy has not been forgotten. Although few survivors remain to tell their stories, a memorial service is held every year to remember those whose lives were lost or shattered. It takes place on Fort Needham, beneath a massive bell tower, on December 6 at 9:05 a.m. And, as a daily reminder, the north face of the city hall clock is permanently stopped at 9:05 a.m.

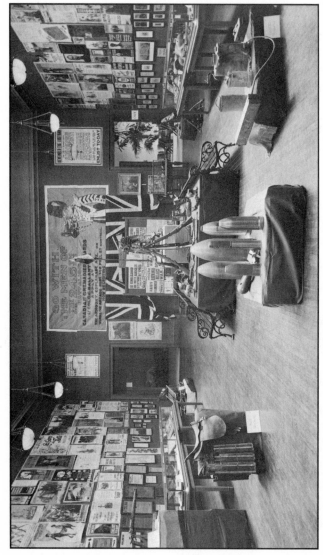

A touring exhibit of war items, including shell casings, recruiting posters, guns and saddles.

The smoke cloud from the blast was visible from far away, as seen in this photo taken from a distance of almost 21 kilometres.

The steamship Imo, *beached on the Dartmouth shore after the explosion.*

Many buildings were flattened into rubble, as this dockside image shows.

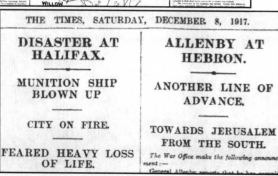

The explosion made headlines at home and abroad. Top to bottom: The Toronto Daily Star, *The Times of London, England, and Ottawa's* The Citizen.

Whole neighbourhoods were flattened or damaged along Campbell Road (later Barrington Street).

Eighty-nine students from the Richmond School on Roome Street were killed in the explosion. Two students died at the school, but eighty-seven of their classmates were killed on their way to school or at home.

Soldiers who were ready to go overseas to fight in WWI were held back in order to assist with the rescue work.

People searching for personal effects, three days after the explosion.

A house lies in ruins following the explosion.

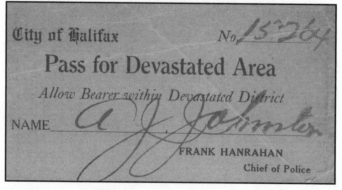

City of Halifax   No. 15264

Pass for Devastated Area

Allow Bearer within Devastated District

NAME _____

FRANK HANRAHAN
Chief of Police

Residents were only allowed into the devastated Richmond area with an official pass.

Haligonians tried to give orphaned children a happy Christmas.

233

Children collecting boxes of food from a relief station.

In the winter of 1917–1918, the only recreation left to many children was sledding.

Temporary Houses

ALL persons rendered homeless by the disaster who will require accommodation in the new houses now being erected, and who have not already applied for one are requested to make immediate application by mail.

The following are the types of houses at present being built:—

per month.

Class "A"—4 rooms and bath: rent $12.00

Class "B"—4 rooms and bath, slightly smaller rooms than Class "A": rent $10.00

Class "C"—3 rooms, no bath: rent . . . .$ 7·50

Class "D"—2 rooms, no bath: rent $5.00

Class "A" houses are at the Exhibition Grounds.

Class "A" and "B" houses on the South Common.

Class "C" and "D" houses on the Citadel Football Grounds.

Kindly fill out the application below and mail it at once.

APPLICATION

Name ....

Former address ....

Number of adults in family ....

Number of children in family ....

Which type of house do you want? ....

At which place do you wish to live? ....

Address to:

J. H. WINFIELD,

Chairman, Rehabilitation Committee, St. Mary's Army and Navy Club, Barrington Street, City.

7269 h 15 m dy 19.

HMS Olympic (sister ship to the Titanic) bringing soldiers back from Europe in 1919. Note the dazzle patterns painted on it.

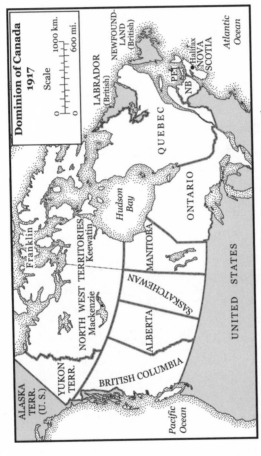

Canada in 1917, when Halifax was a city of 50,000 people.

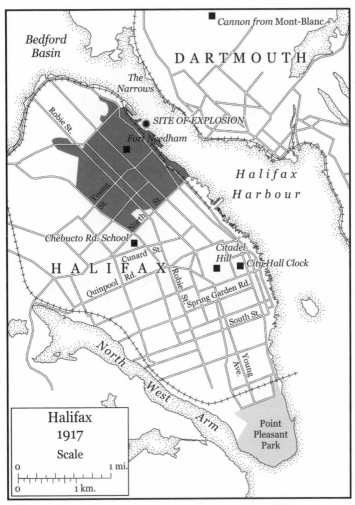

Labels within the map:
- Cannon from Mont-Blanc
- Bedford Basin
- DARTMOUTH
- The Narrows
- Robie St.
- SITE OF EXPLOSION
- Fort Needham
- Halifax Harbour
- Young St.
- North St.
- Chebucto Rd. School
- HALIFAX
- Cunard St.
- Quinpool Rd.
- Robie St.
- Citadel Hill
- City Hall Clock
- Spring Garden Rd.
- South St.
- North West Arm
- Young Ave.
- Point Pleasant Park

Halifax
1917
Scale

0 ——————— 1 mi.

0 ——————— 1 km.

*Halifax and Dartmouth, on either side of Halifax Harbour.
The North End of Halifax (shown by the shaded area) was
almost completely destroyed.*

For Wendy

Author's Acknowledgments

I am grateful to Janet Kitz, author of *Shattered City* and *Survivors: Children of the Explosion,* for sharing her knowledge and offering valuable comments from the very beginning of this project; for reading an earlier version of my manuscript; for giving me a tour of the once-devastated Richmond area; for introducing me to her exuberant Brittany spaniel, Kirsty; and for sharing the harrowing stories of several children who survived the explosion. One such story is that of fourteen-year-old Barbara Orr, who was blown half a kilometre to Fort Needham but lost her entire immediate family — mother, father, three brothers and two sisters.

Thanks to Janet, I was able to interview Edith Hartnett in 2003. Edith, then ninety-four, was nine years old at the time of the explosion. She not only gave me an account of her experiences on December 6, but also painted a vivid picture of her life in Richmond before and after the disaster. Her recollections inspired such story elements as the milk run, Billy the Pig, and the unfinished velveteen dress (in Edith's case, a coat).

Thanks also to the following: Dr. David Sutherland of Dalhousie University, who read the manuscript with an eye to the Explosion and its aftermath; Dr. Desmond Morton, historian and author of such books as *Marching to Armageddon* and *When Your Number's Up: The Canadian Soldier in the First World War,* who answered my questions about the Canadian Expeditionary Force in the Great War; CWO Ray Coulson CD (Ret'd), Curator of the Nova Scotia Highlander Regimental Museum; Rosemary Barbour, Archivist, and the staff of the Nova Scotia Archives and Records; Dan Conlin and staff of the Maritime Museum of the Atlantic; the exceedingly helpful reference librarians behind the "Ask a Librarian" service at Spring Garden Road Memorial Public Library, Halifax; Barbara Hehner for her careful checking of the manuscript; and an enormous thank you to my all-round wonderful editor, Sandra Bogart Johnston.

Acknowledgments

∞

Grateful acknowledgment is made for permission to reprint the following:

Cover Portrait: Detail, from *Girl Holding a Basket of Grapes* by Elizabeth Jane Gardner Bouguereau, courtesy of Brian Roughton of the Roughton Galleries.

Cover background: Detail, lightened, from Nova Scotia Archives and Records Management/NSARM, N-138.

Page 224: *War Trophies Exhibition,* Library and Archives Canada, LAC, C-010166.

Page 225: National Archives and Records Administration, 165-WW-158A-15.

Page 226: Nova Scotia Archives and Records Management/NSARM, N-138.

Page 227: Detail from W. G. MacLaughlan/Library and Archives Canada, LAC, C-019953.

Page 228 (upper): The *Toronto Star* Archives.

Page 228 (centre): The *London Times.*

Page 228 (lower): The *Ottawa Citizen.*

Page 229 (upper): Nova Scotia Archives and Records Management/NSARM, N-201.

Page 229 (lower): Nova Scotia Archives and Records Management/NSARM, N-1263.

Page 230: Canadian Dept. of National Defence/Library and Archives Canada, LAC, PA-022744.

Page 231: City of Toronto Archives, Fonds 1244, Item 1196.

Page 232 (upper): Wallace R. MacAskill, Library and Archives Canada, C-001832.

Page 232 (lower): Nova Scotia Archives and Records Management/NSARM, MG27, Vol. 2, no. 5.

Page 233: City of Toronto Archives, Fonds 1244, Item 626.

Page 234: Nova Scotia Archives and Records Management/ NSARM, N-7081.

Page 235: Nova Scotia Archives and Records Management/ NSARM, Robert S. Low Collection, 1992-524.

Page 236: Nova Scotia Archives and Records Management/ NSARM, MG20, Vol. 530, no. 2, p. 40.

Page 237: Canada, Patent and Copyright Office, Library and Archives Canada, PA-135768.

Pages 238 and 239: Maps by Paul Heersink/Paperglyphs. Map data © 1999 Government of Canada with permission from Natural Resources Canada.

The publisher wishes to thank Garry Shutlak, Senior Reference Archivist, Nova Scotia Archives and Records Management, for checking of images and captions; and Brian Roughton of the Roughton Galleries for his generosity in allowing us to use a detail from Elizabeth Jane Gardner Bouguereau's painting *Girl Holding a Basket of Grapes* as the cover image.

About the Author

Julie Lawson's Nova Scotian roots on her father's side go back to the 1700s. It was her dad who first told her about the Halifax Explosion. *His* father had been there when the explosion happened. "My grandfather, then eighteen, was in Halifax on December 6, 1917, in Victoria General Hospital, waiting to get his tonsils out," Julie says. "When the explosion occurred, the nurses began running down the corridor, holding up their long skirts for greater speed. Grandpa's most vivid impression? The sight of the young nurses' ankles!" (You have to remember that this was in the early 1900s, when women's skirts were quite long.)

"Grandpa died when I was nine, so I was never able to ask him what else he remembered," Julie goes on. "But my curiosity was piqued. I learned as much as I could from my dad, but no mention of the Halifax Explosion ever came up in school, not even in high school history courses. The first book I read about the Explosion was *Barometer Rising,* a novel by Hugh McLennan."

Julie's first trip to Halifax was on an author tour in 1997. A visit to the Maritime Museum of the Atlantic led her to the exhibit *Halifax Wrecked,* which contains numerous photographs, stories of survivors and artifacts. The experience was a potent one. "I was moved by the display of mortuary bags — cloth bags which contained the personal possessions of unidentified victims. Small, everyday things, like a comb, a key ring, a schoolboy's chewed-up pencil, a marble."

One of Julie's library readings on the tour was at the Halifax North Branch, which had on display the Halifax Explosion Memorial Book — an enormous book containing the names of the 1,953 known victims. "For the first time I was struck by the scope of the tragedy on a human scale," Julie says. "The number of victims sharing the same last name was heart-breaking."

A number of things stand out for Julie in the writing of *No Safe Harbour*. One small but surprising research discovery was that between 1917 and 1978, the Halifax Relief Commission had accumulated sixty metres of records! ("No, I did not access them all!" she says.)

But research for the book was often much more poignant. The personal accounts of the survivors were heart-wrenching at times, "but always mesmerizing," Julie says. She would turn to a book to double-check on something, "and find myself still reading an hour later."

Julie was surprised at how quickly the city responded to the disaster, and how fortunate it was that so many soldiers and sailors — in Halifax waiting to be shipped overseas — were not only available, but trained to respond to emergency situations. She was revising the manuscript when Hurricanes Katrina and Rita struck the southern United States during the late summer and early fall of 2005, and found it strangely fascinating to see how the people in another severely devastated area, including soldiers and police forces, handled such a massive catastrophe.

One of the saddest things Julie learned while researching was that the warnings of a second explosion at the Wellington Barracks — an explosion which was feared but never happened — caused both wounded and rescuers to flee from the devastated area, leaving countless victims trapped in burning houses. The result was an even greater loss of life.

Equally tragic was the fact that many Halifax schools were on "winter hours," and school began at 9:30 rather than at 9:00 a.m. Had students already been at their schools, fewer of them might have died, because the schools were more strongly built than most houses. And had students needed to be at school by 9:00 a.m., fewer would have had the opportunity to run down to the harbour for a closer look at the burning ship.

Julie was also horrified to discover that years

after 1917, during the development of the atomic bomb in World War II, scientists went to Halifax to study the effects of the explosion. Their decision to detonate the bombs dropped on Hiroshima and Nagasaki in mid-air, in order to produce a greater range of devastation, was influenced by what they had learned in Halifax.

Writing the diary entries following the disaster was emotionally challenging for Julie, especially since she had grown so close to Charlotte and her family. "I became so immersed in Halifax in December of 1917, that one morning I looked out my office window overlooking the city and saw that all the windows of the buildings had been blown out, leaving empty black holes," she says. "I was stunned, until I pulled myself back to Victoria, 2005, and realized that it was merely a trick of the light."

* * *

Julie is the award-winning author of many books for young readers. Her first Dear Canada book, *A Ribbon of Shining Steel,* was nominated for both the CLA Book of the Year for Children Award and the Hackmatack Award. Her other novels include *White Jade Tiger* (a CLA Honour Book and winner of the Sheila A. Egoff Children's Literature Prize) and *The Ghost of Avalanche Mountain* (nominated for the Silver Birch and Red Cedar Awards).

Among Julie's acclaimed picture books are *The Dragon's Pearl, Emma and the Silk Train, Bear on the Train, Arizona Charlie and the Klondike Kid* (nominated for the Christie Harris Award) and *Whatever You Do, Don't Go Near That Canoe!* (winner of the CNIB's Tiny Torgi Award).

While the events described and some of the characters in this book
may be based on actual historical events and real people, Charlotte
Blackburn is a fictional character created by the author,
and her diary is a work of fiction.

∞

Copyright © 2006 by Julie Lawson.

All rights reserved. Published by Scholastic Canada Ltd.
SCHOLASTIC and DEAR CANADA and logos are trademarks
and/or registered trademarks of Scholastic Inc.

Library and Archives Canada Cataloguing in Publication

Lawson, Julie, 1947-
No safe harbour : the Halifax explosion diary of Charlotte
Blackburn / Julie Lawson.

(Dear Canada)
ISBN 0-439-96930-1

1. Halifax Explosion, Halifax, N.S., 1917--Juvenile fiction.
I. Title. II. Series.

PS8573.A94N6 2006   jC813'.54   C2005-906580-X

ISBN-10 0-439-96930-1   ISBN-13 978-0-439-96930-7

6 5 4   Printed in Canada 114   11 12 13

The display type was set in ChevalierStrSCD.
The text was set in Stempel Schneidler.

∞

First printing January 2006

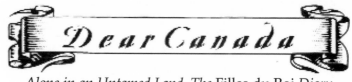

Hoping for Home, Stories of Arrival

If I Die Before I Wake, The Flu Epidemic Diary of Fiona Macgregor by Jean Little

Not a Nickel to Spare, The Great Depression Diary of Sally Cohen by Perry Nodelman

An Ocean Apart, The Gold Mountain Diary of Chin Mei-ling by Gillian Chan

Orphan at My Door, The Home Child Diary of Victoria Cope by Jean Little

A Prairie as Wide as the Sea, The Immigrant Diary of Ivy Weatherall by Sarah Ellis

Prisoners in the Promised Land, The Ukrainian Internment Diary of Anya Soloniuk by Marsha Forchuk Skrypuch

A Rebel's Daughter, The 1837 Rebellion Diary of Arabella Stevenson by Janet Lunn

A Ribbon of Shining Steel, The Railway Diary of Kate Cameron by Julie Lawson

Go to www.scholastic.ca/dearcanada for information on
the Dear Canada series – see inside the books, read an
excerpt or a review, post a review, and more.